“Are yo
he aske
searching her face.

The flare of something in the molten gold was almost as disturbing as the electric sensation sprinting up her arm from his loose grip on her captured wrist.

“No... No, of course not,” she murmured around the ball of something immovable in her throat.

He dropped her hand, but she couldn’t contain the vicious shudder of response.

“Then stand still,” he demanded, but the note of censure was not matched by the light still dancing in his eyes.

She forced herself not to move. And tried not to tremble under that seeking gaze.

“I need a wife, and I am asking you to take the position for a year, at a very generous salary,” he said, his voice so low now it seemed to reverberate in her belly.

A brand-new, spicy duet from Harlequin Presents authors Natalie Anderson and Heidi Rice!

Enemy Tycoons

Sante Trovato and Dario Lorenti's friendship began in an English boarding school, bonded by their Italian heritage—despite their vastly different backgrounds. Until a tragic accident and a deep betrayal tore their bond apart, causing their once-unshakeable friendship to go up in flames, and turning them into bitter enemies...

Years later, the lives of the powerful tech tycoons intersect once again!

Enemies Until After Hours by Natalie Anderson

Tech billionaire Sante is appalled to find his new temporary assistant is his enemy's sister, Mia. But Sante is her boss, so their scorching, forbidden attraction must be contained. Until a storm leaves them stranded together, and the desire they've been denying suddenly ignites!

Boss's Bride Price by Heidi Rice

Ruthless tycoon Dario will do anything to secure his inheritance—even propose a marriage of convenience to the spirited estate manager, Tali, who he was just about to fire! As they head to Sicily for his sister's wedding, Dario's intent on unleashing Tali's long-suppressed sexuality. So long as no emotions get involved...

Both available now!

BOSS'S BRIDE PRICE

HEIDI RICE

Recycling programs for this product may not exist in your area.

ISBN-13: 978-1-335-21368-6

Boss's Bride Price

Harlequin Enterprises ULC
22 Adelaide St. West, 41st Floor
Toronto, Ontario M5H 4E3, Canada
www.Harlequin.com

HarperCollins Publishers
Macken House, 39/40 Mayor Street Upper,
Dublin 1, D01 C9W8, Ireland
www.HarperCollins.com

Printed in Lithuania

USA TODAY bestselling author **Heidi Rice** lives in London, England. She is married with two teenage sons—which gives her rather too much of an insight into the male psyche—and also works as a film journalist. She adores her job, which involves getting swept up in a world of high emotions; sensual excitement; funny, feisty women; sexy, tortured men; and glamorous locations where laundry doesn't exist. Once she turns off her computer, she often does chores—usually involving laundry!

Books by Heidi Rice

Harlequin Presents

Hidden Heir with His Housekeeper
Revenge in Paradise
Billionaire's Wedlocked Wife

Hot Winter Escapes

Undoing His Innocent Enemy

Billion-Dollar Bet

After-Party Consequences

By Royal Arrangement

Queen's Winter Wedding Charade
Princess for the Headlines

Claimed by a Greek

The Heir Affair
Greek's Kidnapped Princess

Visit the Author Profile page
at Harlequin.com for more titles.

To Natalie, a fabulous author
who is always a pleasure to work with!

CHAPTER ONE

'TALI, A LORENTI CORP helicopter landed in the back paddock five minutes ago!'

Tali Whittaker tugged out her earbuds, the old hip hop anthem still buzzing in her head, and propped the pitchfork against the worn wooden door of the horse stall.

'What? Seriously?' She pushed Gracie, the last of the estate's once impressive array of carriage horses, to one side to join her head groom—well, Westwick's only groom now—outside the stall.

She swallowed the bubble of hope as she dragged off her gloves.

Had she heard George correctly? Lorenti Corp had owned Westwick Hall for the past seven years, ever since the last Lord Westwick's death. But his son Dario Lorenti had never used his title, or even his father's surname, and had consistently refused to ever visit the estate when he was in the UK on business.

In fact, she'd never even received an acknowledgement to the many emails she'd sent to the company's head office in Milan in the past two years to ask for more money—after she'd taken on the job of estate manager when the previous manager had quit.

In the past two years, her skeleton staff had worked their

butts off to repair what they could and keep the place running on a shoestring. But the profit they made from the agricultural side of the business, the glamping field they opened during the school holidays and the house tours, tearooms and events they hosted each weekend were not enough to pay for the upkeep of the Hall itself. Six hundred rooms of history and grandeur, the Georgian stately home hadn't seen any significant investment for a decade, and it showed. Her staff were depending on her to make Westwick a success, but she'd felt the weight of that responsibility ever since she'd come to work here as the last estate manager's admin assistant as soon as she'd finished Sixth Form college, age eighteen. And the thought that she was failing them, and failing Westwick, had been keeping her awake at night now for months.

'Yes! Lorenti was in it! He's here, *finally*, Tali!' George's craggy face lit up with excitement. 'I saw him and a number of suits get out of his chopper.'

The bubble of hope expanded and threatened to cut off Tali's air supply.

'He still has a limp,' George said, because like Tali he had met Lorenti once before, when the Lord's son had spent months recuperating at Westwick Hall after a terrible car accident which had nearly killed him. Tali pushed down the memories which still came to her in dreams sometimes. Visions of that surly, moody seventeen-year-old moaning in pain in the huge four-poster bed and shouting at her mother in Italian. Her mother had been responsible for the boy's care as the new housekeeper—and had told Tali not to bother him.

But Tali had been eight and left to her own devices for most of that summer—plus she'd overheard her mother telling one of the maids she thought 'the poor boy' was lonely. So Tali had made it her mission to visit him over the following weeks, even though he'd shouted at her in Italian at first, too—the same way he'd shouted at everyone. He had fascinated her, like the wounded animals she brought into her mum's cottage on the estate and tried to heal… Plus his dad didn't seem to want him. He and his sister hadn't even come to live in England until their mother died in Italy… And they'd never lived at the Hall until he had come to stay that summer.

In all those weeks, Lord Westwick had only visited him once. It gave them something in common, Tali had thought at the time—because her own dad hadn't wanted her either, once he had his 'new' family.

'You should go.' George grabbed the pitchfork, still beaming, as a surge of panic joined the balloon of hope in Tali's chest.

'Crap.' She stared at her jeans and flannel shirt. She was covered in horse manure. Did she have time to change? She wanted to make a good impression—she had so many things she needed to tell Lorenti about the estate.

'You best hurry, Tali. He'll want to talk to you first,' George added, then hesitated, his voice becoming pensive. 'Do you think he'll remember you? You became such friends that summer.'

'I doubt it, George,' she said, not wanting to hope. They hadn't been friends, not really. He'd been a teenager and her just a child. Plus, he'd been a captive audience, because until the very end of the summer he was too broken to even get out of the bed.

She knew he'd seen her as an irritation at first, then a useful distraction, her attempts to befriend him an escape from the pain of his injury—and eventually, a way to relieve the boredom of his long recovery.

Tali had heard the staff and her mother mentioning his only friend had caused the crash and then left him on the roadside to die. When she'd asked Dario if that were really true—because who did something so mean?—he'd growled something in Italian and then sulked for days. So, she hadn't asked again.

That he'd never come to Westwick Hall since his father's death seven years ago though, or replied to her emails, was also a pretty big clue that he didn't remember the little girl who had hovered around him all summer trying to bring him out of his shell. She certainly didn't intend to rely on their past association now to get him to invest in the Hall. Because that would be totally unprofessional.

She rushed out of the stable and raced across the courtyard and around the Hall's main building, heading towards the annexe, which had once been the carriage master's cottage, where the estate office and her tiny flat above were situated.

Finally, she had a chance to pitch all the ideas she had to Dario Lorenti to improve the Hall's revenue and make everyone's job here more secure—which had been her mission since day one.

Lorenti was a billionaire by all accounts. He had money to burn. And it made absolutely no sense to let his greatest asset rot, even if he didn't want to live here.

She skidded to a stop when she rounded the corner, finding a short, older man standing at the office door with a scowl on his face.

'Hi, I'm Tali Whittaker,' she said, realising this must be one of the suits George had mentioned arriving with Lorenti.

'Signora, I am looking for the estate manager. Signor

Lorenti is waiting,' he said in perfect if heavily accented English, his tone clipped.

'Right, of course,' Tali began, trying not to feel too disappointed about having to kiss her shower and power suit goodbye.

She'd just have to make a great impression in her muddy jeans.

'I'll come with you…' she started.

The impatient man interrupted her. 'Signor Lorenti only wishes to speak with the estate manager. You must direct me to him immediately.'

Him? Seriously?

So Lorenti had never even *read* her emails.

'You're looking at him. Or rather her. *I'm* the estate manager,' she said.

The man's eyebrows rose as his gaze flicked over her. Heat blitzed her cheeks.

But then he nodded. 'Let us go. Signor Lorenti has been waiting long enough.'

Tali allowed a spurt of irritation to cover the sting of hurt as she followed Lorenti's judgy minion into Westwick Hall and up to the Hall's library on the second floor, where Lorenti had been waiting to speak to her…for all of ten minutes. While she had been waiting for years to *finally* speak to him.

CHAPTER TWO

WHILE LORENTI'S ASSISTANT knocked on the library door and waited for a reply, Tali brushed off her clothing, tied her long hair into a knot at the back of her head and swallowed the lump of panic.

She was young for her position at twenty-two and not looking her best at the minute. But there was nothing she didn't know about the estate. She'd lived here almost as long as she could remember, ever since her mum had taken the job of housekeeper after her dad had deserted them both—the winter before Lorenti's accident.

She just hoped she didn't have any horse manure on her face.

'Entrare.'

The lump pushed into her throat at the harsh demand delivered from behind the door.

The assistant opened the door and introduced her in Italian.

Tali plastered what she hoped was a professional smile on her face as she stepped into the room.

She inhaled the smell of old leather and lemon polish, comforting and familiar, as the assistant excused himself and closed the door behind him on his way out.

She'd always loved the library—the rows and rows of

books, many of them first editions, displayed on shelves that rose two storeys and included a mezzanine level accessed by a wrought iron spiral staircase. At the far end of the room was the old Lord's mahogany desk. Behind it stood Lorenti, with his back to her, as he gazed out of the large, mullioned window, which looked out over Westwick's circular driveway and the fishing lake beyond.

Lorenti's silhouette in the light cast by the mid-morning sunshine made him seem incredibly tall, his muscular shoulders and lean waist displayed to perfection in a steel grey designer suit. His stance was tense, making the usually soothing atmosphere in the library bristle with energy…

The lump of panic expanded. Should she alert him to her presence?

He raked his fingers through his hair, the waves cropped close to his head. His hair was much shorter than she remembered it being that summer, when it had grown long enough to hit his collar.

She shook her head to dispel the distant memory. And gave herself a mental kick.

He's not that wounded, angry teenager anymore. He isn't going to remember you, and you don't want him to. Because you're already at enough of a disadvantage... first-impressions-wise.

In fact, he seemed to have forgotten she was there, transfixed by who-knew-what in the driveway… She hoped it wasn't the potholes they'd been unable to afford to fill in this spring.

The moments ticked past, the grandfather clock by the door keeping time with the hammer thuds of her pulse—and increasing the tension which hovered around him like an aura.

She cleared her throat. 'Mr Lorenti, you wished to speak to me…urgently.'

He stiffened as if he'd been woken from a trance, then turned. Even in the half-light she could sense his gaze on her. The energy emanating from him seemed to stroke her skin, then sank into her abdomen. The heat in her cheeks blasted to her hairline.

'*Vieni qui…* Come into the light,' he demanded. The brittle tone made her shiver.

She stepped forward with as much courage as she could muster under that penetrating stare—which seemed to look through her without seeing her.

'*Che cosa?*' he murmured.

'I'm sorry, I don't speak Italian,' she managed, wondering if he even realised he'd spoken in his native tongue. She'd been trying to learn Italian on an app over the last two years, in case anyone from Lorenti Corp came to Westwick, but she wasn't confident enough to converse in it yet.

He frowned. 'Who are you?'

'I'm Westwick Hall's estate manager. Your assistant said you wanted to speak with me?'

Now that he was no longer in shadow, she could see his face, and it wasn't helping the swooping sensation in her stomach. His features were sharper and more dramatic now, having lost the softness of youth—but his eyes, that rich dark brown flecked with molten gold which held so many secrets, were exactly the same… The scar on the left side of his face was also still there, slashing across his cheek all the way to his hairline. But where the scar had been disfiguring that summer, the livid bruising and stitching fresh, now it only made him look more striking.

Something else about him, though, was *very* different. Or maybe she simply hadn't noticed it when she was eight—and a child, instead of a woman. The combination of those harsh features, his magnetic eyes and his tall, muscular build made him look incredibly…*hot*…

She dragged in a breath. No, *hot* was too basic—more like *breath-taking.* Her stomach fluttered, annoyingly.

She'd never been the type to swoon over good-looking guys, because they usually turned out to be egotistical arseholes. Not that she'd ever met any who were *as* good-looking as this man.

She mentally kicked herself. Again. *Hard.*

So what if Dario Lorenti's rugged male beauty—accentuated by that designer suit and the dark scowl on his face—was making her light-headed. He was still technically her boss.

Plus, while she'd never been interested in celebrity gossip, Joss and Becca—the Hall's cleaners—had told her all about Lorenti's playboy reputation, because they were celebrity news junkies. So, even if he looked like every woman's fantasy, he really wasn't.

It also became clear he was nowhere near as impressed with her appearance when his eyes narrowed, and his gaze swept over her grubby clothes.

'How old are you?' he demanded, his tone as searing as the inspection.

'I'm twenty-two,' she replied firmly, trying not to sound defensive.

One dark brow lifted. 'How can you have the experience to run a large estate at this age?'

She winced at the judgemental tone and the note of criticism.

The truth was, although she'd worked for two years as the previous estate manager's assistant and taken courses at the local agricultural college in project management, she *didn't* have the experience. But that was hardly her fault.

'When Mr Chambers quit two years ago, no one else would take the job at the reduced salary we could offer,' she said. 'And Lorenti Corp didn't respond to any of my emails outlining the problem.'

She shoved her hands into the back pockets of her jeans, to stop them trembling.

This meeting was not going how she'd hoped. Why was he being so hostile? And why did she get the feeling his harsh expression wasn't just about her lack of qualifications?

'So, I stepped up to the role as an interim arrangement,' she finished.

And maybe if you'd replied to a single one of my emails you would know all this already.

The muscle in his jaw tensed, making the scar on his cheek flex. But then the flecks of gold in his irises shimmered, his gaze intensifying as if he was seeing her properly for the first time. 'What is your name?'

'Tallulah Whittaker,' she blurted out, not sure why she'd given him her full name.

Everyone called her Tali, because she had never felt like a Tallulah. The florid, old-fashioned name had belonged to her father's grandmother, and she'd always considered it just another burden her dad had saddled her with—along with his disinterest, and the crippling bouts of sadness which had dogged her mother for years after he'd walked out on them.

But the formality of her proper name felt like a trusty shield against Lorenti's disapproval.

His eyes narrowed even more as he studied her.

Suddenly, heady recollections of the brooding, unhappy

teenager whose enforced solitude she had insisted on disturbing that summer swirled through her consciousness.

Should she tell him they had met before?

Perhaps he hadn't completely forgotten the little girl who had worked so hard to entertain him that summer. But as he continued to stare at her, his inscrutable gaze made her palms start to sweat, still buried in her back pockets. And it occurred to her this meeting was already awkward enough, without bringing up ancient history. Plus, if she had ever known that boy, she certainly did not know the man he had become.

At last, he nodded. 'I suppose your qualifications are of no significance now,' he remarked.

What was that supposed to mean?

The swooping sensation in her stomach went into overdrive when he walked to the desk and lowered himself into the chair. The pronounced limp had sympathy tangling with the knot of anxiety in her stomach.

Was he still in pain? His movements were stiff, unwieldy, but his face no longer had the strained, stoic pallor she remembered from the early weeks after his accident, whenever the painkillers had worn off.

He opened a laptop on the desk, jolting her out of her thoughts.

Stop staring at him and thinking about that boy and start making a better impression on your boss.

Gathering a breath, she launched into the spiel she'd rehearsed a million times in the last two years, during all those sleepless nights, preparing for this exact moment.

'Actually, I'm so glad you're finally here, Mr Lorenti,' she began, determined not to falter when his gaze rose to hers, the blank disdain even more intimidating than the sceptical frown. 'There's so much to discuss about Westwick. I've worked up a detailed investment plan to turn the Estate around. It's got so much potential, and our hiring freeze is only the tip of the iceberg when it comes to problems with staff…'

'Fermare.' He held up his hand.

She stopped talking, intimidated despite herself by the command in his voice. The lump of panic became a boulder. Something was seriously wrong.

'Your plans are not important now, Tallulah Whittaker,' he said, the hollow tone of voice somehow much worse than the earlier hostility. 'As I am here only to end your employment. The land will be parcelled up and sold as soon as possible.' He glanced around the room, his features devoid of emotion, while Tali's stomach went into free fall—and the boulder threatened to crush her ribs.

At last, that searing gaze landed back on her face. 'And the Hall demolished.'

CHAPTER THREE

'BUT? *WH-WHAT?* Y-YOU CAN'T... You can't do that, Mr Lorenti.'

Dario stared at the girl standing in front of his desk, her chest heaving with emotion under the shapeless plaid shirt, her striking blue eyes bright with—were those tears?

He stifled the ripple of something hot and fluid, which had hit him the minute she had stepped out of the shadows and into the light.

She was hardly the sort of woman he would ever consider dating, with her dirty work clothes, her mess of caramel curls tied back in a haphazard knot, her soft, pale skin devoid of make-up. Not only did she look too young for the job she had inherited, clearly by default, she looked too young to date anyone. And certainly too young for a man like him, even if she was telling the truth about her age.

The frustration which had propelled him to this godforsaken place today—thanks to the fallout from his disastrous meeting this morning in London with the Westwick Estate's board of Trustees—swept through him. And resentment blindsided him again.

After seven years of negotiations between Lorenti Corp's legal team and the Westwick Trustees who controlled his mother's old home on Capri—the palazzo he had spent a small fortune renovating and restoring since his father died—those bastards had refused point blank to let him bypass the terms of his father's will to inherit the palazzo outright.

He ground his teeth, furious that he had been unable to circumvent the demands his father had made from beyond the grave—in seven long years of legal wrangling.

It had always struck him as a cruel joke that his father had allowed him to inherit Westwick Hall, a place he had always hated, while keeping the palazzo in trust—until he agreed to marry an Englishwoman. But after trying to force those old fools to see reason through the courts, he wasn't laughing anymore.

But he refused to let his father win.

The bastard had always railed against the fact his only son and heir considered himself an Italian. That Dario had never given a damn about fitting into the mould of an English gentleman so he could inherit the Westwick title and estate. His father had cut him off when he was eighteen to try to force his hand. But instead of capitulating, Dario had borrowed money and built a hugely successful tech business, managing to amass his own fortune without any help from his father.

The terms of his father's will had been Lord James Westwick's last-ditch attempt to bring Dario to heel, by keeping ownership of the palazzo—which contained the only memories he had of his mother—out of Dario's hands unless he married an English debutante.

Seven years ago, when he'd first heard that blasted will, Dario hadn't been concerned. He'd simply set his legal team to work on breaking it… Unfortunately, the ancient aristocratic friends his father had put in place were as entitled, old-fashioned and intractable as the bastard himself, and had stymied every one of Dario's attempts to purchase the palazzo without marrying anyone.

While also spending a large portion of the Westwick trust to fight him in court.

He hadn't cared, because he didn't need or want his father's money. But the irony—that he owned Westwick Hall, a place he didn't want, while he would never own Palazzo di Constanzo now—had only fuelled his fury. That fury had propelled him here for the first time in fifteen years, to decide what to do with the Hall, which he had been ignoring since his father's death.

Receiving an invitation to his sister Mia's wedding while en route here today—she was marrying that Sicilian bastard Sante Trovato, the man who had once abandoned him on a roadside and left him for dead—had added another layer of fury to his frustration.

The fact he would have to attend the wedding only increased his anger. If Mia was foolish enough to fall for that man's dubious charms, so be it. She had made it clear only a few weeks ago she did not value Dario's counsel. She had also refused to accept a penny from him over the years, even though she had been cut off by their father too, her blasted independence so precious she would rather starve than admit she needed his support. But as her older brother, it was his duty to make one last attempt to get her to see Trovato for who he really was. Which meant Dario was going to have to attend the event on the man's private estate in Sicily in two weeks' time. The hasty wedding was also a red flag as far as he was concerned.

If he managed to stop himself from killing his sister's fiancé, it would be a miracle.

But the invitation had helped Dario make a decision about what to do with Westwick Hall. He would sell off the land and raze the house to the ground. Then at least he would have had payback for his father, if not Trovato, for their attempts to destroy him.

Take that, you old bastard!

He hardened his heart against the genuine look of horror in his estate manager's translucent blue gaze.

'There is no need to become hysterical,' he remarked, because she looked as if she were struggling to draw breath. 'You and your staff will be paid six months' severance which you will not have to work for, as I will close the house for good this weekend.'

He wished to find a buyer promptly for the land. Of course, he could have sold the house too. Even in its current state it was probably worth millions. But the resentment that had lived inside him for so long—and had built to a tsunami this morning—meant that demolishing it felt like the perfect revenge for being prevented by his father's Trustees from owning the palazzo.

'Please don't do this!' The girl stepped forward and pressed her palms on the desk. 'You don't know what you're doing. You have no right. Westwick is a part of history, it's a…'

'I assure you I have every right,' he said, as evenly as he could manage while his resentment was threatening to choke him. 'This isn't personal,' he lied.

'But it makes no sense. Why would you destroy something so beautiful?' she asked, the agony in her voice giving him pause.

Apparently, this *was* personal, to her. He let his gaze drift over her again. That strange prickle of memory disturbed him, but not as much as the liquid pull of arousal. Her shirt was open, allowing him to see the tops of her breasts.

'You may think it beautiful.' He levered himself off the chair and walked back to the window, the ache in his bad leg helping to control the spike of lust. 'I, on the other hand, do not.'

'But it's on the English Heritage Registry, you can't just demolish it.'

Dario swung round. 'What does this mean?'

'The Hall's historic significance means it's an important part of the nation's heritage. They could bring charges against you…'

'Puttana!' The full force of Dario's anger and frustration returned in a rush.

Then I will close it up and let it rot...

But as he glared at the girl, who was shaking visibly, her arms wrapped tightly around her midriff, the threat got caught in his throat.

It was what he had felt in his heart ever since inheriting the place seven years ago. A place he hadn't visited since his teens, when he had been locked up here for months, the pain in his leg nowhere near as agonising as the pitying glances of the staff, and the pain in his heart… At his best friend's—his *only* friend's—betrayal.

But he was no longer that damaged boy, vulnerable and alone. Yes, his leg would never be fully healed—the pins used to repair the crushed bones had saved it, but only just. But he'd hardened his heart, not just against Sante, but also against anyone else who might betray him—or pity him—again.

'If you'd just let me outline the plans I have for Westwick,' the girl began, her voice quivering with emotion, 'you'll see it can more than make the money back that needs to be spent on it to restore it to its former glory.'

He frowned at the girl.

Former glory? Was she mad?

Westwick Hall had never been glorious. Not to him. He still remembered the first time he had come here, age thirteen, after his mother's death. It had been cold and miserable that day, the ground muddy underfoot, the clouds cutting out the weak sunlight which had no warmth, even in May. His sister had clung to his hand and looked as lost as he'd felt, while the father they didn't remember, his face contorted with disgust, had shouted at Dario to speak in English—a language he barely understood.

Capri and his mother, and the life he and Mia had lived on the island with her throughout his childhood—free to roam as they wished—had seemed a million miles away that day, as well as in the weeks and months and years afterwards, when they had both been parcelled off to different boarding schools, forced to remain in this dreary country.

There had been no more early mornings scrambling down the path to the palazzo's private lagoon, to go swimming in the sparkling blue waters. No lunchtimes spent begging leftovers from the kitchen staff for him and Mia, while the housemaids cleared up the previous night's mess. No more lazy afternoons spent sailing or fishing, or in the wintertime messing around on his computer, gaming and teaching himself to code. And no evenings spent feasting and dancing and falling asleep under the stars while their mother and her many flamboyant cosmopolitan friends partied until sunrise.

Gabriella Lorenti hadn't believed in rules, and hadn't

believed much in schooling either, but she'd loved him and Mia unconditionally.

Their childhood had been precarious at times, scary even, when the men his mother loved to entertain became surly, or possessive. Sometimes, Dario had wished for a little less wildness, a little more sleep, a little more security for Mia—who had quickly become as headstrong and impulsive as her mother. But when he'd come to England, to the cold and the damp, and been forced to live under strict pointless rules, forced to adhere to a punishing school schedule and learn an ugly language, made to spend hours each day reading and writing about old Englishmen when it was the codes and numbers he loved…then he had realised how much more he had lost than just his mother's flamboyant hugs, her endless chatter, the vivacious personality which made it exciting just to be near her.

England was lifeless and tasteless, sterile and suffocating and dull. Much like his father and this godforsaken pile of stone.

But clearly the girl didn't feel the same way, because she was staring at him with desperation in those cornflower-blue eyes.

'Please, Mr Lorenti, if you'll just give me a year. I've itemised everything in my budget. It would mean a small increase in our running costs and some capital investment, to make the necessary repairs and improvements, but we could more than make it back.'

He tuned out the request. But the something he had been trying to ignore ever since she'd stepped into the light spiked in his gut again. And with it came an idea. The same idea he had dismissed seven years ago when he had first heard the terms of his father's will…

He had been determined then not to bow to his father's

demands. And not just because he had hated the man's attempt to manipulate him, but also because he had decided never to marry anyone. He simply did not have it in him to trust another person that much. Nor did he wish to care for anyone again the way he had once cared for his mother, and Mia, and even Sante, all of whom had abandoned him.

His advisers, of course, had suggested an arranged marriage early on to satisfy the Trustees. But until this moment he had refused to consider the suggestion. He had never dated a British woman and did not know any members of the English aristocracy, because he had never used his title nor taken up the seat left vacant by his father in the House of Lords. His life was in Italy. But if he couldn't demolish this place to get his revenge on his father, perhaps there *was* another way…

'Are you English?' he asked.

The girl blinked, confused by the question. 'I'm… Yes, I was born near here. But I have British and Irish passports as my mother was born in Dublin.'

The feeling in his gut surged. Even better then—with an Irish passport she could live in Italy with him as long as was necessary to convince the Trustees he had abided by the terms of the will.

To hell with it. He'd been wrestling with this situation for seven years. And the decision to wreak vengeance today on his father, and the stately home he had cared about more than he had ever cared for his children, would have given Dario some satisfaction, but it would not have given him what he truly wanted—his name on the deeds of Palazzo di Constanzo. And frankly, where was the satisfaction in besting a dead man?

'If I save the house from demolition, and consider your proposals for the estate, I will need you to do a job for me in return,' he said. 'One I would pay you handsomely for,' he added, because he required this to be a business transaction first and foremost. He certainly did not want this girl getting any romantic notions about the arrangement. She was young, and clearly not wealthy, and her emotional investment in what was just a job was a sign she was also naïve and sentimental.

'Absolutely, Mr Lorenti, but I really don't need a pay rise. I'd rather put any additional money into the repair budget.' A tentative smile curved her lips, her relief palpable as her pale cheeks took on a rosy glow. 'But you could give *everyone* a pay rise at the *end* of the year, if you're satisfied with the work we've done,' she finished, clearly trying to temper her joy at his sudden turnaround. 'Which I guarantee you will be.'

Yes, she was definitely naïve, he realised, and far too trusting. She hadn't even heard yet what he was going to ask of her. But her trusting nature only made this arrangement more perfect. A cynic would be more likely to realise their bargaining power.

'The job I am referring to has nothing to do with your work as my estate manager…'

Her eyes widened. The deep blue of her irises shimmered—her confusion tangible. The wary expression reminded him of a young doe he had once had in his sights while hunting with his mother's gamekeeper as a boy many years ago in Amalfi.

'It…it doesn't?' she whispered.

He hadn't been able to pull the trigger and kill the young deer that day. He couldn't, because the creature was so beautiful. And so defenceless. And he'd been less ruthless as a boy. But he had no qualms about pulling the trigger now.

'I require an English wife for a year.' That should be long enough to fool those old bastards into transferring ownership of the palazzo—and while his father had clearly intended for him to marry an aristocrat, there had been no specific reference to his bride's social status in the will. 'If you agree to take the job, I will pay you two million euros as a divorce settlement, in a year's time.'

CHAPTER FOUR

'I... I BEG your pardon, Mr Lorenti?' Tali murmured, sure the emotional roller coaster ride she'd been on since entering the library had just crashed off the rails.

That surge of awareness wasn't helping her keep a grip on her cognitive faculties either. She couldn't possibly have heard the Italian billionaire correctly.

If he needed a wife—for a year—which was peculiar enough, why would he ask *her*? Not only did he not know her from Adam, but she was also so far from being his type she might as well be circling Mars.

She worked on a farm! Her mother had been his father's housekeeper. She'd been literally shovelling horse shit less than fifteen minutes ago, some of which was still decorating her jeans. And she'd never even read about the sort of events and parties and soirees—were soirees even still a thing?—that men like him would attend, let alone been invited to one.

'You heard me correctly, Tallulah Whittaker,' he said, using her full name again, but this time caressing the vowels with that husky Italian accent, almost as if he were mocking her.

Okay, great, now she'd dropped wholesale into another

dimension. One in which Dario Lorenti found her amusing, instead of beneath contempt.

Unfortunately, that only made her reaction to him more disturbing.

The heat in her cheeks fired across her collarbone and reached past her aching lungs to tighten her nipples into hard peaks.

She folded her arms more firmly across her chest, attempting to get a grip.

'Are…are you joking?' she asked, not knowing why he was making fun of her, but trying to see it as a good thing. At least with that cynical smile on his lips he didn't look so forbidding.

Whatever was going on with him, she had to negotiate it diplomatically, or he might reiterate his threat to demolish the Hall, which would leave her staff—all of whom she considered to be her friends and her responsibility—out of work and her and, even worse, her mum homeless. Elsa Parker had worked long hours as a housekeeper here ever since Tali's father had abandoned them both. And when she'd decided to take early retirement a year ago after a bout of bursitis, Tali had promised her mother she could remain in the cottage she'd lived in for the past fifteen years. Her mum still helped out in the tearooms at the weekend, so the peppercorn rent she paid was totally justified, in Tali's humble opinion. And losing her home might break her mum again, the way she had been broken after Tali's father had left, which was another reason why Tali would do everything in her power to save Westwick.

'A simple yes or no will do,' he said as he stepped around the desk, his limp doing nothing to make him seem any less intimidating, until he stood in front of Tali. Close enough for her to inhale the scent of clean woodsy soap, blended with the refreshing hint of citrus and sea salt in his cologne.

She tried to step back, aware she probably didn't smell anywhere near as delicious, but he reached out and clasped her wrist to prevent her retreat.

'Are you scared of me, Tallulah?' he asked, those rich brown eyes searching her face. The flare of something in the molten gold was almost as disturbing as the electric sensation sprinting up her arm from his loose grip on her captured wrist.

'No…no, of course not,' she murmured, around the ball of something immoveable in her throat.

He dropped her hand, but she couldn't contain the vicious shudder of response.

'Then stand still,' he demanded, but the note of censure was not matched by the light still dancing in his eyes.

She forced herself not to move and tried not to tremble under that seeking gaze.

'I need a wife, and I am asking you to take the position for a year, at a very generous salary,' he said, his voice so low now it seemed to reverberate in her belly.

'Why do you need a wife for a year?'

And why would you employ me when you've dated tons of much more suitable women who'd do the job for free?

She bit into her lip to stop herself from voicing *that* question, because it felt far too personal.

His brows lowered, his gaze became shuttered and the muscle in his jaw twitched again, signalling his disapproval.

'The purpose of this arrangement is not your concern,' he said. 'Do you understand?' There was that note of command again, and condescension, which was playing havoc with the weightless sensation in her belly.

Was this really happening? Because this whole situation had begun to feel like a weird anxiety dream, which she was hoping she would wake up from soon.

'I… I guess so,' she said, even though she didn't understand at all.

'So, what is your answer, Tallulah? Two million euros for a year of your time.'

'I—I don't want the money,' she said, making his brows snap together. 'For myself…' she added quickly, because she could see he wasn't happy with that response either. 'But if you would consider investing in the Hall as soon as possible, so I could give the staff a pay rise and start putting my plans for the business into action, I'd be happy to consider it… But I'd need a few guarantees first.'

If the Hall could become profitable, instead of just barely sustaining itself, Lorenti would surely want to invest more, and all the people who relied on her for employment—people she cared about—would have their futures secured, too. But she needed to clarify what the position he was offering her entailed before agreeing to more.

What would a man like Dario Lorenti even require in a wife? What exactly was he expecting her to do, and for a whole year? It sounded like a public position. But the way he was looking at her, with that dark intensity in his eyes, was making parts of her ache that had never ached before—and that could not be good…

'What guarantees?' he snapped. The business-like tone, though, helped to stop the hot rock in her chest from vibrating… Unfortunately, it did nothing to shrink the one which had become lodged between her thighs.

'Well, like, what do you want me to do? *Exactly?*' she asked, feeling breathless again.

The cynical smile twisted, but he seemed unfazed by

the question when he replied—his tone practical and pragmatic. 'You would marry me, after you sign a pre-nuptial agreement, as soon as possible. Then you would need to do everything I request to make this marriage appear genuine—in public.'

The breath she had been holding released in a rush. So this was a stunt marriage.

He let out a low chuckle. 'There is no need to look so relieved, Tallulah, that I am not proposing a genuine marriage.'

The blush blazed across her chest and blasted into her cheeks. Was he amused or offended? 'I'm sorry, I didn't mean to imply…' Her heart raced into her throat. 'I mean, I'm sure you're very appealing to women.' The blush burned as one dark eyebrow arched.

For heaven's sake, Tali, shut up!

'But *you* do not find me appealing?' he prompted.

'It's not that, I just, I…' She swallowed, the hot rock between her thighs calling her a liar, but the constriction in her lungs winning. 'I've only just met you… And I work for you. I don't think it would be appropriate for us to…to…'

She trailed off.

Sheesh, why don't you just dig a hole in the carpet and jump into it.

'For us to *what*, Tallulah? Exactly?'

She heard the hint of sarcasm then and saw the renewed spark of amusement in the golden brown.

He was mocking her. The…*bastard*!

She breathed through the flash of temper.

Dario Lorenti was a powerful and ruthless man who held her future and the happiness of the people she loved in the palm of his hand, and who had no scruples about using that power to get what he wanted. Trying to appease him probably wasn't the best strategy, because it was like playing peek-a-boo with a tiger. Eventually, she'd lose.

She had no idea why he needed this fake marriage, or why he had picked her, but she had to ensure she didn't allow him to beguile and belittle her. No easy feat, given she didn't have a lot of experience with men generally.

She wasn't a virgin. She'd dated at school and gone all the way with a boy she'd met at agricultural college… But those pleasant if not particularly memorable encounters hadn't got her anywhere near as hot and bothered as Dario Lorenti had with a single look.

Sexual confidence seemed to ooze from this man's pores, and he used it as a weapon, without even trying. Because how else had he put her whole body on high alert—every pulse point pounding, each erogenous zone humming—when she was fairly sure she didn't even like the guy? And she certainly did not trust him. He was far too surly, and mercurial, and unreadable. And that was before you factored in that he was proposing they 'pretend' to be man and wife for an entire year…

Stop acting like an airhead then! And talking in silly euphemisms.

'I don't think it would be a good idea for us to sleep together!' she blurted out, seizing the tiger by the tail. 'If I take on the role of your wife, that's all it would be, a role. I just want that understood. In case you were wondering…'

His eyes narrowed, but what she saw in them bolstered her resolve—not amusement anymore, but admiration.

'Duly noted, Tallulah,' he murmured, his ego clearly not dented by her assertion, but at least he wasn't laughing at her anymore. 'What we choose to do in private would not be part of your paid role as my wife,' he continued.

'Okay, good,' she said. His phrasing was a little weird, because they wouldn't be doing *anything* together in private, surely. But English wasn't his first language, and she was glad he wasn't going to press the point, because the hot spot between her thighs had begun to ache.

'You will take the job then?' he asked, although it didn't really sound like a question, his confidence as intimidating as everything else about him.

'I… I suppose so,' she said. His eyes flashed with that exhilarating intensity, forcing her to add, 'But I'd need the money now.'

Westwick was falling apart, and her staff hadn't had a pay rise in years. She couldn't wait any longer to secure the investment they needed.

Irritation doused the fierce glow in his eyes at her counter demand. Clearly, he wasn't used to being bargained with. But she refused to cower or back down. If she was going to spend a year having to appear in public with this man, and dealing with all these bizarre tingles and pulses, not to mention his controlling and volatile personality, she had to make sure it would be worth it. But the truth was, pretending to love, honour and obey him would be a small price to pay to secure the Hall's future—and make all her dreams for her dream job become a reality.

'I will put five hundred thousand euros into the Hall's operating account *once* you have signed the pre-nuptial agreement,' he countered. 'And a further five hundred thousand on the day we are wed. The balance of the investment, though, will be contingent on your ability to adhere to the terms of our agreement—and will *not* be paid until I am entirely satisfied with the outcome of this arrangement.'

Tali blinked, the heat rising in her cheeks—and a few

other disconcerting places besides—at the commanding tone, but right alongside that disturbing reaction was the giddy burst of hope.

A million euros! It was more than she could ever have hoped for when she walked in here—and that was before his initial threat to demolish the place. Even if Lorenti wasn't satisfied with the arrangement—which she suspected he wouldn't be, when he discovered she was about as far from being trophy-wife material, even *fake* trophy-wife material, as it was possible to get—the Hall would have a million euros of new investment.

She could repair the holes in the roof and the driveway, give everyone a modest pay rise, fund the tearoom's much-needed makeover and offer their chef Jim a full-time job—so he could give up the night shifts at the local pub she knew he hated. Plus her mum's home would be safe and Tali could even begin the infrastructure projects that would demonstrate to Dario Lorenti the magnificent potential of the stately home he had inherited.

It was all good. In fact, it was fantastic. And if by some miracle she managed to pull off the role of trophy wife to Lorenti's satisfaction—which was a very big if, but she'd do her best—they would have an additional million euros to play with in a year's time. Of course, it would help if she had some idea of what he was trying to achieve with this fake marriage, why he needed it and why on earth he had chosen her, but that could wait until she knew him better.

The thought of spending more time in his company made the strange reaction in her abdomen pulse and glow, alongside the giddy leap in her heartbeat. She ignored it.

This was a job, he'd said so himself. Lorenti was a fascinating man—and okay, beyond gorgeous. But he was also scarily intense and unknowable, and she suspected that would never change, no matter how much time she got to spend with him over the coming year—which would probably only be a few strategic appearances together, she hoped.

She could still remember the taciturn and angry teenager, whose moody façade she'd only managed to make a few dents in as a little girl. And he'd been a great deal more vulnerable and approachable then—lonely and in pain—than he was now.

She'd been a lot more naïve herself as an eight-year-old, of course, convinced all Dario Lorenti had really needed was a friend, someone to make him smile, someone to care about him, to help him heal. She'd strived to be that person once, but it would be like butting her head against a brick wall now, and she'd done enough of that as a child, trying to get her father to notice her.

What all those ignored texts and emails had taught her, eventually, was that you couldn't change people, and you couldn't make them care about you if they chose not to. So, it was pointless to try.

Even so, her heartbeat thundered in her ears when Dario murmured in a gruff voice, 'Do we have a deal, Tallulah Whittaker?'

She nodded. 'Okay, I'm in,' she replied, trying to focus on the million euros and all the things she could do with it, and not the unreadable expression on his harshly handsome face—which was making her pulse points go haywire.

He held out his hand. 'Let us shake on it.'

She reached out, but as his hand gripped hers, something fierce and shocking leapt up her arm and surged into her sex.

His eyes widened a fraction, as his fingers tightened.

Had he felt it, too—that shocking burst of adrenaline

which was even now causing her legs to feel like overcooked noodles and her lungs to contract?

If he had, he controlled it faster than she could, the flecks of gold in his irises mesmerising her as he lifted her hand to his lips in a practiced move. But before his mouth could connect with her knuckles, he sniffed and dropped his gaze to her fingers.

Humiliation engulfed her as she became brutally aware of what he could see, and smell. The dirty, broken fingernails, the rough calluses, the scent of sweat and horses and manure.

His grasp loosened and she tugged her hand free. She closed her grubby, work-roughened fingers into a fist and hid the offending hand behind her back.

She braced herself, the swift kick of vulnerability almost as disturbing as the crippling disappointment. Would he withdraw the job offer, now that he had incontrovertible proof of how unsuitable she was to play his wife?

But instead of breaking their deal, his sensual lips lifted in the first genuine smile she'd seen on his face. The light dancing in his eyes turned the gold flecks to molten magma.

'You have forty-eight hours, Tallulah, to make yourself presentable,' he said, his tone more amused than judgemental. But as the string of orders continued, Tali's relief proved to be short-lived. 'My legal team will arrive today. You must sign the pre-nuptial agreement before we meet in Milan to announce our engagement in two days' time. I will arrange a separate apartment for you there, while we attend events as a couple. But at the end of the following week, we must travel to Sicily for my sister's wedding,' he continued, the dispassionate tone comprehensively obliterated by the purpose in his eyes which seemed to detonate in Tali's sex. *What the hell?* 'I will tell Aldo to make all the necessary arrangements and assist you over the coming days.' He walked back around the desk, but then his gaze skimmed over her. 'He can start by arranging a manicure.'

She wanted to be outraged at his high-handedness and that dictatorial tone. But how could she be, when she'd totally signed up for this? What bothered her more, though, was the schedule he'd outlined so dispassionately.

It was all too much, way too soon.

'But I can't join you in two days. I'll need more time to get my assistant Ellie up to speed here. And I can't spend a fortnight in Milan, especially if you then want me to travel to Sicily with…'

He held up his hand, halting her babbled plea in mid-babble.

'Are you reneging on our deal so soon?' he asked, one brow lifting ominously.

'No, but I'm needed here. Ellie's good, but she's never handled everything on her own. Exactly how long would we be in Sicily…?'

'That is not your concern.' He cut her off, making the panic threaten to choke her. He didn't look amused any-more, his scarred cheek clenching, signalling his irritation. Unfortunately, he wasn't the only one getting annoyed. 'You will be with me whenever, and wherever, and for as long as I require,' he added.

'But…' she tried again.

'This is not a negotiation, Tallulah. Either you accept these terms, or I close the Hall as planned and investigate how to have it demolished…'

The threat felt like a knife to her gut, but she couldn't quite control her own temper. He was being unreasonable.

And she wasn't even sure why. What on earth would she be doing in Milan for close to two weeks?

'But I can't just abandon my staff…' she said, the anxiety making her lungs hurt. 'I've never been away for more than a weekend.' The truth was, she hadn't taken a full day off work in the last two years, and she had never had the chance to travel… She was pretty sure her day trip to Calais at school didn't count. But he didn't need to know any of that, because he had far too much information on how unsophisticated she was already—thanks to broken-nail-gate.

One of the things she loved most about her job at Westwick was the sense of purpose and achievement it gave her. She'd always been industrious and hard-working and, as much as she'd hated seeing the Hall's decline, she'd also adored the challenge of running a place of this size and complexity on a shoestring.

She'd feel utterly useless in Milan twiddling her thumbs, and hideously guilty. Because how on earth were her already beleaguered staff going to manage everything without her?

Lorenti was utterly unmoved by her pleas. His features set in the stony expression of disapproval she had become familiar with in the past twenty minutes. But then, to her surprise, as he stared at her, the muscle in his jaw stopped clenching.

'For this to work, I expect you to be available to me at all times,' he growled, his voice husky with intent.

Tali tensed, the wave of heat which flushed through her shocking in its intensity. 'But I…'

'Hear me out,' he interrupted her again. 'If you wish to continue your work here during the year ahead, I will allow it. Up to a point.'

Allow it!

'I… I do wish,' she managed, feeling like a rabbit in the headlights of an oncoming juggernaut. And not just because he was being such a dictatorial jerk.

She wanted this deal to go ahead, so Westwick would have a future, but the shocking heat flushing through her system like a tsunami made her feel as if her whole life—and everything she had ever known about herself—was being swept away before her eyes.

'Then you may continue your work here in person,' he said. 'When I do not require your presence at my side. Otherwise, you can oversee your responsibilities via the internet. And hire any extra staff you feel appropriate, at my expense. This is my final offer.'

She could see he meant it.

A part of her wanted to tell him she couldn't accept—that she couldn't be his fake wife for a whole year if it meant spending weeks away from the estate. Westwick was more than a job to her. This place made her feel valued and safe, and it always had, ever since she'd first arrived as a child. It was where she'd recovered from her father's rejection, and where she'd helped her mum eventually heal her broken heart.

And while another part of her knew she couldn't throw away this chance to give Westwick the lifeline it so desperately needed… What if saving Westwick Hall and the estate—and looking after all the people who depended on her—wasn't the only reason she wanted to say yes?

Lorenti was demanding and scarily intense, and pretending to be his wife, even in public, was going to be much more of a challenge than she had originally anticipated. But she also knew he had always intrigued her.

And agreeing to do this felt weirdly exhilarating as well as intimidating.

While she knew this arrangement wasn't personal for him—despite those devastatingly intense looks, which he probably sent to all women—leaving Westwick, agreeing to see new places, to do new things, would push her way outside her comfort zone. And maybe she needed that, just a little.

Until this moment, she hadn't realised that in many ways she'd been hiding here. Her non-existent love life since college was a case in point…and quite possibly the only reason she was so ridiculously susceptible to those intense looks.

She sucked in a breath and went with her gut instinct, instead of succumbing to the panic making her throat hurt. 'Okay, I guess I can live with that.'

He nodded, then opened his laptop. 'Then I will see you in Milan in two days' time,' he murmured gruffly.

She turned to go, determined not to be hurt by the curt dismissal. But as she walked out of the library on unsteady legs, she felt weirdly like a completely different person than she had when she'd walked in here—could it really have been less than thirty minutes ago?

She was nowhere near as sure of herself and her place in the world, but maybe she was also a bit less artless and gullible and unsophisticated.

Which had to be a good thing. Because handling this dangerous man and his demands, possibly for a whole year, felt fraught with a lot of risks…

Even if it got her the reward she'd hoped for, for so long.

CHAPTER FIVE

Two days later

'SIGNOR LORENTI WILL be here at six to escort you to the opera, Signora Whittaker. The stylist and her team will arrive at four to dress you.'

Another stylist! Seriously?

Tali tried not to scream, or look ungrateful, but after forty-eight hours of being prodded and poked and told what to do, she was utterly exhausted. And frustrated… And closing in on feeling completely overwhelmed.

She'd arrived in Italy less than an hour ago—on Lorenti Corp's private jet, which had been disconcerting enough—and then been taken in a chauffeur-driven car to this penthouse apartment, which Lorenti owned in Milan's Brera district.

As the car had wound its way past the cobbled alleyways flanked by historic terraces built in an eclectic mix of Renaissance and Baroque architectural styles, she'd spotted luxury boutiques side by side with bustling sidewalk cafes and upscale food emporiums. The artsy crowd frequenting them had looked as chic and stylish as their surroundings—and intimidating to a woman who had barely been out of Wiltshire in the past five years.

She hadn't needed Aldo to tell her this area was one of the most exclusive in the city. The luxury furniture and sleek, expensive design of the huge penthouse apartment, which would be her home for the next ten days, and the colonnaded stone balcony beyond, were even more intimidating.

She wished she could be more grateful. But she felt so far out of her depth at this point, and so anxious and stressed, it was hard to appreciate anything—least of all a visit from *another* stylist in less than two hours' time.

The last two days had been endless rounds of appointments with hairdressers, and beauticians, and fashion buyers, and stylists, as well as all the meetings Lorenti had warned her about with his legal team—who had begun to arrive at Westwick Hall less than an hour after she'd made her devil's bargain with Lorenti, and he'd left.

She had been buffed and plucked and waxed and dressed to within an inch of her life while busy being informed about what Lorenti required of her, and reading and signing a ton of legal documents. In between all that, she'd barely had the time to prepare Ellie and the rest of her team for her sudden departure—not to mention to explain to everyone at Westwick, without lying *too* much, exactly what was going on with her and Lorenti. And why she was suddenly leaving for Italy for who knew how long.

Her mum, of course, had refused to buy the love-at-first-sight story which she had hastily concocted—and which had fooled the staff.

'This happened in the space of half an hour? Really Tali, I know he's a handsome man, and you were always fascinated with him as a little girl, but that doesn't sound like a good basis for a relationship, honey.'

Tali had been forced to come clean about the deal she'd

struck with the Hall's owner—and then sworn her mum to secrecy. Because the very first form the legal team had insisted she sign, before the sixty-page pre-nuptial agreement even, had been a non-disclosure agreement forbidding her from divulging to anyone that her marriage to Lorenti was not genuine.

'*Grazie*, Aldo,' Tali said as she dropped her bag onto the living area's expensive four-seater sofa. That would be the battered rucksack she had packed with a few clothes of her own, to wear in her downtime, when she wasn't wearing the four suitcases sitting in the hallway full of carefully co-ordinated outfits the London buyer had supplied her with.

'Do you know what opera we're seeing?' she asked, trying to drum up some enthusiasm for the night ahead…and not freak-out completely at the thought of seeing Lorenti again when she already felt overwhelmed.

She'd never been to an actual opera. Surely tonight would be exciting, once she stopped stressing about how everyone at Westwick was going to cope without her, and whether her mother would keep the secret she'd entrusted her with long enough not to get them both sued. And how on earth she was going to persuade any of the glamourous, stylish people Dario Lorenti probably socialised with in Milan that he would choose to marry a farmgirl from Wiltshire?

'I do not, Signora, do you wish me to find out?' Aldo asked, looking apologetic. Lorenti's assistant—who had been so impatient during their first meeting—had turned out to be surprisingly helpful, carefully co-ordinating her many meetings and appointments in the last two days, so she'd had at least some spare time to do her *actual* job.

'Don't bother.' She sighed. Or rather, what *she* considered to be her actual job, even if Lorenti had made it very clear during their one meeting that Westwick Hall was no longer her priority. Because being at his beck and call was her job now…

Buck up, Tali, you're just stressed and confused and hopelessly out of your depth. You'll adapt, you always do. And this is only for a year. Securing Westwick's future is worth it.

Although after forty-eight hours of being at Lorenti's beck and call—without him even being in the same country—she was beginning to realise what an enormous commitment she'd signed up for. Who knew being a fake trophy wife would be this much work? And all of it so utterly vacuous and unfulfilling—because since when was getting your eyebrows threaded or trying on hundreds of designer outfits a viable job?

'It'll be a nice surprise,' she added.

'Shall I request the apartment's chef make you a meal before you leave?'

'There's a chef?' She searched the state-of-the-art kitchen on the other side of the open space—scared a cordon bleu chef was about to jump out and intimidate her even more.

'Yes, Signora. Your staff live in the rooms below.'

My staff? There was more than one person to wait on her. *Oh god!*

The anxiety which had been making it hard to breathe for days contracted around her lungs like a vice.

'I requested they leave you to rest,' Aldo said gently. 'But if you would prefer to eat…'

'No, Aldo, I'm good, really. I'm not hungry.' Because… Nerves! 'I'm just going to crash until the stylist arrives. You've been amazing. I really appreciate all your help over the last few days.'

The man went a dull shade of red. 'It is my job, Signora,' he said, before giving her a stiff bow and leaving.

Good to know one of us has a proper job.

She stared after Aldo as the apartment door closed. Had she embarrassed him? She hadn't intended to. But she guessed this was just another example of how ill-suited she was to the role Lorenti had hired her for. She knew precisely nothing about navigating this level of privilege, even though she'd grown up on the grounds of a stately home.

Chill, Tali. Having a personal chef isn't scary... It's just a bit much. You'll get used to it...eventually.

Kicking off her shoes, she wandered to the balcony and opened the ornate glass door to step onto the cool marble tiles of a huge terrazzo. Propping her elbows on the stone balustrade, she peered across the rooftops towards Milan's Centro Storico nearby—and spied the cloistered splendour of the Palazzo Brera art gallery in the neighbouring square which Aldo had pointed out when they'd arrived. She took a moment to ease her breathing, control the anxiety and absorb the sights and sounds of this beautiful, vibrant city.

This was an adventure. She had never been to Italy before, and while the Milanese were intimidatingly chic, she would need to find a way to relax and enjoy this experience—or she'd end up having a heart attack. Plus, Ellie had her on speed dial if she needed her. She'd managed to hire Ellie an assistant which Lorenti was paying for, *and* she planned to check in with the Hall's new acting estate manager every single morning.

She still had no idea why Lorenti had picked her for this job, and maybe that was what was stressing her out. Unfortunately, thinking of Lorenti brought back the memory of his turbulent gaze, and the sensations which had sprinted up her arm and deep into her belly the first—and only—time he had touched her.

She shivered, despite the warmth of the spring day, and folded her arms around her body, then headed into the apartment, intending to take a shower—a cold one.

This was a fake marriage. He and his legal team had made that very clear. He didn't want more, nor would he, and neither did she. And while the thought of seeing him again in a few hours' time was making the inappropriate heat in her abdomen glow alarmingly and kicking her stress levels back into the danger zone, surely their first public appearance would be a good opportunity to start establishing their working relationship. And stop her fixating on the weird physical response she'd had to him in the library—which had to be a layover from all the other emotions he'd bombarded her with that afternoon. And nothing whatsoever to do with the awareness in his eyes, which she was convinced now had all been in her far-too-vivid imagination.

Dario used his key fob to enter the penthouse apartment he owned across the square from his own residence, annoyed by the buzz of anticipation in his gut, which must surely be a symptom of his unprecedented reaction to Tallulah Whittaker two days ago. It was a reaction he had spent the last forty-eight hours determined to quash.

He tucked his hands into the pockets of his tuxedo pants, aware of his accelerated heartbeat—not to mention the warmth in his abdomen—at the thought of seeing the girl again.

Assurdo!

What on earth was the matter with him? He had hired the girl on a whim, to fix a problem which had been weighing on him for seven years. Nothing more. She had intrigued him—her passion for her job, that sheen of naivete which clung to her, and her obvious awareness of him—more than she should. Perhaps because his encounters with women over the years had become so jaded, her unguarded reactions had been refreshing. But while she was undeniably pretty, her eyes a striking blue which had reminded him of the sea in Amalfi, her figure had been hidden beneath shapeless clothes, and her appearance hardly remarkable.

Two older women appeared, carrying a garment bag and a box of cosmetics. They must be the team Aldo had hired to prepare Tallulah for her debut as his fiancée tonight.

'Signor Lorenti,' one of them said, sending him an enthusiastic smile. 'Your fiancée is waiting for you on the terrazzo. She wished for some air before your arrival,' she added, her gaze skating over him, the appreciative twinkle one Dario had become accustomed to from women, young and old, despite his ruined face.

'Congratulations on your engagement,' the other said. 'You will make a very striking couple tonight.'

He gave them both a curt nod as they let themselves out of the apartment, oddly ambivalent at the news of Tallulah's transformation.

He had told Aldo to hire the best stylists and beauticians in the business in both London and Milan to ensure his 'bride to be' would look the part tonight—so he should be glad to hear they had done their job. The engagement announcement had been released two hours ago—with some concocted story about them becoming acquainted on his non-existent trips to his family estate in the UK over the past two years—so there would be no going back on this arrangement.

Even so, a confusing sensation joined the weight in his gut as he walked towards the apartment's terrazzo—anticipation.

He dismissed the sensation, which reminded him unhelpfully of being a young, untried boy on Capri besotted with the beautiful models and actresses who had frequented his mother's parties.

He stepped onto the terrace and spotted the young woman standing with her back to him, staring into the sunset. The blue satin dress, which stopped far too high up her thigh, seemed to mould to her bottom, displaying it like an offering, while the jewelled heels she wore made her toned legs look about a mile long.

The idea of those legs wrapped around his waist turned the anticipation to harsh, desperate need. He breathed through the intense reaction.

She wore a matching jacket, her hair piled on top of her head and held with an array of jewelled pins. Diamond earrings sparkled in the dying sunlight. No doubt they matched the ring in a box in his jacket pocket which the stylist had sent over that morning, but which he hadn't even looked at.

Just props, to make this engagement appear real.

He coughed, to alert Tallulah to his presence, his throat so dry it felt like sandpaper.

She spun round, clutching a small purse. The jacket had no buttons, revealing the gown's bodice, a concoction of satin and transparent lace which cupped her breasts—drawing his attention to the petal-soft skin of her cleavage, far too much of which was on display.

Che cazzo?

Raw desire burst through his veins—like a river in full flood, swelling the heat in his groin and making him stiffen with a devastating combination of shock, awe and possessive fury.

Although the cocktail gown was undoubtedly stylish, it was nothing short of indecent. Tallulah Whittaker had been transformed from the artless girl he recalled—in muddy jeans and a shapeless shirt—into a sex goddess to rival La Loren herself in her heyday.

What the hell had the stylist been thinking, dressing a woman who belonged to him in an outfit that would display her charms to every other man within a ten-mile radius?

Except she is not yours, Lorenti. This is just for show.

The voice of reason whispered in his head but was drowned out by the thunder of blood in his ears, which was heading south so fast it was making him light-headed.

'Mr Lorenti,' she murmured, her voice unsteady, unsure. 'Is everything okay?'

Her lips glistened in the twilight as she spoke, painted with some kind of gloss. The fierce desire to cover that wide mouth with his and thrust his tongue deep made his temper flare alongside the lust.

He marched across the terrace, only vaguely aware of the stiffness in his leg.

She blinked, the glittering make-up on her lids making her wide eyes look even bigger and more guileless. The deep blue of her irises matched the clinging fabric of her dress, which seemed even more indecent the closer he got.

He paused. The shocked awareness on her face reminded him of that artless girl in battered jeans and a shapeless shirt. Her wide-eyed reaction and the familiar grinding pain in his leg were enough to contain the fire in his gut from burning out of control…*just.*

'You don't like the dress?' she asked, clutching the purse

too tightly, then bit into her bottom lip, sending another devastating shaft of heat to his already heavy cock.

He forced himself to breathe, and stop glaring, although he could not be held responsible for the furrow on his brow which was fast becoming a crater.

'It is more revealing than I expected,' he said, on a growl of disapproval.

She tensed as if she'd been struck.

And his anger returned. Although he knew the cause of his displeasure wasn't only disapproval of her attire, or not precisely. That would have been so much easier to handle. No, he was glowering at her because of the dawning realisation that he was going to struggle to keep this relationship professional for a week, let alone a year. The urgent, animalistic desire barely concealed by his tux jacket had already made him lose sight of what this damn arrangement had been supposed to achieve.

'It's not appropriate for the opera?' she asked, her concern obvious as she glanced at the dress and smoothed a trembling hand over the short skirt.

Fuck the opera! I don't wish anyone to see that much of you, except me.

The reply roared in his head, but he managed to prevent it from flying out of his mouth, barely aware not only that it would sound deranged, but that it was also unprecedented. Since when did he give a damn how much skin his dates had on display?

Concern shadowed her wide blue eyes, while her lip trembled.

He ground his teeth to get a grip on his reaction.

This wasn't her fault. She hadn't picked the damn dress—that would have been the stylist he'd paid a small fortune for.

'I'm sorry, I didn't…' she mumbled, looking panicked. 'Madame Rosa said this style is all the rage. Do you want me to change?' she asked. 'There's about a thousand other dresses in my luggage. I'm sure I can find something less revealing.'

But as she went to rush past him, he clamped a hand on her wrist. Raw sensation ricochetted up his arm, reminding him of when he'd touched her before. And the spark of arousal flared. *Terrific.*

'Wait,' he grunted, his tone sharp with demand, as he struggled to control his febrile reaction. 'There is not time.'

He could make time, of course. He owned a corporate box at the opera house, and if they arrived late, it would only make their story more convincing. Everyone would assume he had been availing himself of his fiancée's undeniably spectacular charms. But the violent need coursing through his system made it clear to him that he had to get out of this apartment. Because controlling the yearning to discover exactly what was under that damn dress was already tormenting enough.

'Are you sure? It's no trouble, Mr Lorenti. It's not really my style anyway…'

'Yes, I am positive…' he snapped, his temper fraying, along with his self-control. Then he noticed the pulse pumping against the delicate well of her collarbone.

What would it feel like, to kiss her there? How would she react, if he feasted on the thin skin, and marked her as his for every other man to see?

'And stop calling me Mr Lorenti, Tallulah,' he added.

She stiffened at the harsh tone. He released her wrist and tried to gentle his voice.

'We are supposed to be engaged, the press release went out hours ago,' he managed, trying to contain the burst of temper, and the vision which had popped into his head unbidden and was only making matters in his pants even more pressing, literally. 'You must call me Dario.'

'Right, sorry, Mr Loren… I—I mean Dario.' She dipped her chin to her chest, the blush highlighting her cheeks, making him feel like a brute. 'I'm making a mess of this already.'

The defeated tone and the unnecessary apology finally pierced the haze of lust. His rampaging heartbeat slowed—slightly—as well as the fierce flow of blood charging beneath his belt.

Damn it, Dario. Stop behaving like an arsehole. None of this is her doing.

She did not even appear to realise the effect she was having on him.

'There is no need to apologise,' he managed.

He tucked a knuckle under her chin and raised her gaze to his. The feel of her skin was so soft, he had to force himself to drop his hand, instead of stroking her neck, and tracing a line through her cleavage, to circle the hard bud of her nipple pressing against the satin.

'You have done nothing wrong.'

She nodded, although he could see the wary, guarded expression and knew she did not believe him.

Dio, what was happening to him? He prided himself on always keeping his emotional responses on lockdown, of being sophisticated, cynical and self-reliant. He *never* let anyone see the side of him which had once struggled to contain those emotions. As a boy, he'd been far too needy, far too desperate for friendship and affection after his mother's death. It was why he had attracted people like Sante, who were only too happy to exploit him. But it had always been remarkably easy not to care, not to need anyone after Sante's betrayal…

Until this precise moment.

It is of no importance. This is lust, pure and simple. Something that will be easily contained—once it has been satisfied.

Because it was already obvious that his unprecedented reaction to this woman would have to be satisfied eventually. He'd never experienced such a strong physical connection to a woman. But he had no intention of satisfying it yet, not when he was so on edge—barely clinging onto the cast-iron control he had always relied on during his past relationships.

There was no doubt in his mind, he and Tallulah would sleep together—her lust-blown pupils, engorged nipples and catapulting pulse making it clear she was no more immune to this volatile chemistry than he was.

He had sensed it in Wiltshire but had tried to deny it. Partly because he had no desire to make this arrangement any more complicated than it had to be, but mostly because he had never been led around by his cock before.

He enjoyed sex. A lot. He always had. He was a workaholic and considered it a valuable—and time-efficient—way to relax. As a result, he considered himself a generous and accomplished lover. The women he dated had certainly never complained about the physical aspect of their relationships. Of course, he'd been accused of being cold, and insensitive to their emotional needs, but as soon as that became an issue, he considered it his cue to end the relationship. What some women had failed to believe, once he had dated them more than a few times, was that he genuinely had no desire for any kind of intimacy beyond the physical.

Unfortunately, though, dumping Tallulah once they had

satisfied this hunger would not be so easy, because he had employed her to pretend to be madly in love with him… for a year.

Once they had burned out this firestorm of lust, he would end their private relationship, but ending their public one would be impossible—until he had persuaded the Westwick Trustees he had adhered to the terms of his father's will. And knowing how damn contrary those old fools were, he doubted that would happen to his timetable.

All of which meant he would have to manage this situation, so that when he and his fake wife *did* become intimate, Tallulah did not misconstrue their sexual connection for something more.

The possibility that their livewire chemistry might have contributed to his impulsive decision to employ her as his wife in the first place could not be discounted now. The lowering thought was sobering enough to give him some relief from the insistent heat building in his pants.

'The car is waiting downstairs,' he said, determined to get her out of the damn apartment before the respite evaporated.

But when he placed his hand on the small of her back, to direct her out of the apartment, her shiver of reaction echoed viciously in his groin.

As they travelled down in the apartment's private elevator, with her looking subdued, and him straining to recapture his usual control, he grimaced at the thought of the night ahead…when he was going to be forced to watch *La traviata* with her in a private box and persuade everyone that they were already lovers, all while figuring out how to make her his lover for real, without screwing up the whole purpose of this relationship.

The brutal irony did not escape him.

But far worse was the challenge of pretending to be a besotted lover—already a stretch for a man like him, who did not have a romantic or flirtatious bone in his body—while unrequited desire was pounding in his groin like a jackhammer, and the scent of wildflowers which clung to her was threatening to send his senses into another tailspin. And that was without even factoring in the extremely tenuous hold he already had on his temper, as he imagined every single man in the Teatro alla Scala being treated to a virtually uninterrupted view of his new fiancée's breasts.

As he watched the tiny skirt ride up even more of her thigh as she entered the waiting limo, he bit his tongue to contain the renewed wave of possessive fury—and raw hunger—and made himself a promise.

First thing tomorrow morning, Madame Rosa was getting fired.

CHAPTER SIX

TALI SETTLED INTO the shadowy interior of the chauffeur-driven limousine, aware of Lorenti's forceful—and disapproving—presence as he folded his tall frame into the seat beside her.

Clearly, she'd screwed up with the dress. Or rather, Madame Rosa had, because his reaction to it had been nothing short of disastrous. His gaze had been more searing on the apartment balcony, when she'd turned to find him standing behind her—looking totally devastating in the black tux—than it had been forty-eight hours ago in Wiltshire. But with none of the humour.

The nerves in her stomach tangled. Had she ever felt more hideously out of place in her entire life? She certainly didn't think so. And she wasn't talking about the butt-skimming skirt or the semi-see-through top of her opera outfit.

The truth was, she'd been horrified too, when she'd first seen what Madame Rosa was proposing she wear for the evening. The expensive designer couture was so unlike her usual style—which always leaned towards comfort and practicality. Even on the rare occasions when she took a night off work to go to the local pub she usually just shucked on a clean pair of jeans and a nice shirt. But an opening night at Milan's legendary opera house was hardly quiz night at the Talbot Arms—so she had sucked up her discomfort and agreed to the stylist's suggestion.

But once she'd seen her reflection in the mirror and Madame Rosa and the beautician Clara had complimented her profusely on her appearance, the knot in her belly had dissolved at least a little, despite her nerves.

Maybe she didn't look like herself anymore, or the self she had always known, but the smoky, professionally applied eye make-up, the gleaming lip gloss, the gown's chic style and expert detailing, the diamond drop earrings which dangled against her neck, the elaborate chignon the hairstylist had managed to tease her insane curls into… and those elegant heels! All of it had the wow factor, even she could see that… She'd felt exposed, sure, but also like she might have some chance of persuading Milan's finest that Tali Whittaker had somehow caught the eye of a man as successful and compelling as the city's foremost tech billionaire. So there was that.

But then Lorenti had arrived and instead of being wowed too by the efforts of the designer and the beautician and the hairdresser, he had looked startled and then… well, outraged. His gaze had raked over her, and those rich chocolate eyes had gone dark and stormy with discontent.

She'd been crushed, the anxiety tying her guts back into hard, greasy knots. Not least because his volatile reaction had also made the hot knot in her belly—which seemed to always be there whenever she was in his company—sink even further into her sex.

But as the chauffeur closed the door and the car drove off into the nighttime traffic, the bristling silence that reverberated around the luxury leather interior like a physical force had her crippling embarrassment and confusion giving way to dismay…and irritation.

Lorenti had hired *her* to do this job. He'd even hired the stylist and the beautician and the hairstylist, or at least he was paying for them. In ten minutes—traffic allowing—they were going to have to pretend to be madly in love. And yet he was sitting on the opposite side of the car staring broodily out of the window at the crowds of stylish Italians, refusing to even look at her. Sulking, basically. If he wanted this arrangement to work, he was going to have to meet her halfway. He moved effortlessly through the circles of Europe's elite—the people he was expecting her to impress—people whose lifestyle she knew sod-all about. If he wanted to persuade any of them she was his chosen bride, he was going to have to help. Because no way in hell could she pull this off on her own.

She cleared her throat to dislodge the lump of anxiety and forced herself to take the bull by the horns.

'I'm sorry if you hate the dress, Mr Lorenti. But you're going to have to look at me—and pretend you don't hate it, and me in it—when we get to the opera. Or no one on earth is going to believe you want to touch me, let alone marry me.'

He turned towards her. His eyes flared, the chocolate brown turning to a molten gold. But weirdly what she saw in his gaze wasn't the contempt she'd expected…but something much more confusing—and frankly, dangerous.

'I told you to call me Dario,' he said, but the clipped command was softened by the husky tone. His molten gaze coasted over her exposed skin like a physical caress and turned the weight between her thighs into a boulder. A very hot boulder. 'And the issue is not that I hate the dress, but that I like it far too much.'

Finally, his gaze landed on her face, the heat in it as searing as the sensation now pulsing between her thighs.

'No one will believe I do not wish to touch you, when the problem I currently have is how I am going to stop myself from stripping you out of that damn dress during three solid hours of opera.'

'Oh…' she murmured, shocked not just by his directness, and the harsh appreciation in his expression, but how it made sensation flare across her skin like wildfire. 'Well, I guess that's a good thing then. That it won't be hard for you to pretend to…'

'I will not be pretending.' His lips twisted in a rueful smile that was almost as exhilarating as the heady leap in her heart rate. 'But it will definitely be hard,' he said, the deliberate double entendre somehow diffusing the tension, while also ramping it up to fever pitch.

Her gaze dropped to his lap entirely of its own accord. And she spotted a bulge in his lap, barely disguised by the loose-fitting suit trousers.

Leaning across the seat, he tucked a knuckle under her chin and lifted her gaze away from the evidence of his reaction. 'Be careful, Tallulah, or I may test my resolve right here in the limousine.'

She blinked, aware of the flush scouring her cheeks. The erotic promise in his eyes was so potent, she crossed her legs instinctively—which instantly made matters worse, when the pulsing between her thighs became catastrophic.

'And that would be bad?' she murmured, the cheeky challenge coming out before she could stop it.

His brows lifted, and she knew she'd surprised him again, which felt oddly empowering. But then his lips curved. The urbane, arrogant smile was matched by the feral light in his eyes—which carried an erotic threat so potent the pulsing in her panties got worse.

'That would be up to you,' he said as his thumb trailed down her neck. The tantalising caress eased over her throat as she gulped, traced her collarbone, then dipped to skim across her breast and tease the tight bud of her nipple.

She gasped, the brutal dart of sensation at the light touch making her swollen clitoris throb so hard she was astonished she didn't pass out.

'Tell me you wish to explore our chemistry, Tallulah, and we can forget about the opera.'

Oh, yes please.

The thought blasted into her brain, but right behind it was the surge of panic when he added, 'But be aware, it would change the terms of our arrangement. As once I have had you, I very much doubt I will want to let you go for a while.'

The dark determination in his eyes, and the way his thumb continued to toy with her nipple, had the urge to say yes getting locked in her throat.

Even through the delicate fabric, his touch felt so sure, so certain, so confident. While her response—the urge to arch her back and offer him more—was so wild and instinctive it scared her.

Sleeping with Dario Lorenti would push her even further out of her comfort zone. What did she know about the sort of sexual liaison he was talking about? Even less than she knew about Europe's cultural elite, frankly.

And that was before she factored in her incendiary response to his slightest touch.

The driving need, the desperate hunger felt far too needy—and completely out of her control. Because she didn't know him. Plus, she was still anxious about being able to fulfil the role he was *actually* paying her for. Adding sex to the mix wouldn't exactly simplify the situation… And it was unlikely to cure her performance anxiety either, given he was clearly a lot more experienced than she was. Despite the enormous bulge in his pants, he didn't seem to be anywhere near as on edge. This would still be just an 'arrangement' to him. And while a part of her knew becoming his stunt wife with benefits would help make their charade more convincing—would she still feel like a stunt wife if she slept with him, given that she was so much less jaded and worldly than him?

She covered her breast with a shaky palm, and his touch dropped away.

'I… I don't think that would be a good idea,' she managed.

Or at least not yet, her needy body qualified. Not until she was sure she could control her emotions, the way he seemed able to control his so effortlessly.

Staying out of Dario Lorenti's bed—especially if he continued to look at her as he was now, as if he wanted to devour her in a few greedy bites—was going to be an even bigger challenge than persuading Italian high society he would pick *her* to be his wife.

Instead of looking annoyed, or even irritated, he simply nodded. 'As you wish, Tallulah.'

That harsh, heady gaze remained on her burning cheeks though, as he reached into his jacket pocket and produced a velvet box.

'But there is something that I want you to understand…' he continued.

He flipped open the box, revealing a beautifully crafted silver ring with a diamond solitaire in the centre. The gemstone glinted in the lights from the passing streetlamps as the car inched through the traffic towards the opera house.

Lifting the ring out of the velvet, he discarded the box.

He took her trembling fingers in his and slid on the exquisite engagement ring. It fit perfectly, because of course it did.

'Whatever you decide, Tallulah, you are mine now, until the conclusion of our arrangement,' he said. 'And I will not allow you to wear something so revealing again…' Those dark eyes met hers, the erotic promise becoming a tantalising erotic threat. 'For anyone but me.'

She shuddered, her throat drying to parchment at the authority in his voice, her nipples so hard now they could probably drill a hole to China.

She should tell him he was only paying for her cooperation in public, that he had no right to dictate what she wore in private—for him or anyone else. But she couldn't seem to unstick the words from her throat. Because no man had ever looked at her like that before. As if the only person he could see in that moment was her.

But when he lifted her fingers to his lips to brush a kiss across her knuckles, the heat in her sex rose to wrap around her heart, and she trembled violently.

As soon as he released her, she buried her fist in her lap, the delicate ring heavy on her finger, her skin burning where his lips had touched.

This wasn't a real engagement any more than it would be a real marriage—whatever they decided to do in private. So why did his possessive statement feel so compelling, as well as completely outrageous?

Tali, get a clue.

As the car stopped on the historic opera house's courtyard, the breath Tali had been holding expelled from her lungs.

She could see the photographers through the tinted glass, crowding around the red carpet laid out on the cobbled stones for the opening night. The Teatro alla Scala's elegant and imposing façade dated back to 1778. All of Italy's greatest composers had presented their work here, from Puccini to Verdi to Toscanini, she'd discovered while investigating what they would be seeing tonight on the internet. But somehow, as she stepped out onto the red carpet, and watched Dario buttoning his tux jacket to disguise the erection she'd caused, the flashes from phone lights and camera lenses, the questions shouted in Italian from the local celebrity hacks eager to ask about their 'engagement' and the thought of seeing her first-ever opera, were nowhere near as overpowering as the feel of Dario's large palm resting on her back. Or the fierce need having a field day in her panties. Or the sparkle of the diamond engagement ring on her finger which was supposed to be a prop for their fake marriage but now felt more like a mark of his ownership.

CHAPTER SEVEN

Ten days later

'THE FEATURE WRITER is with Signor Lorenti, Signora Whittaker,' Aldo announced as Tali stepped from the lift into Dario's palatial apartment.

She smoothed down the demure skirt-and-blouse combo the new stylist had recommended for the interview with Italy's top-selling glossy women's magazine. It didn't do much to control her rampaging heartbeat though. She'd been stressing about this interview ever since Aldo had informed her it had been set up two days ago.

Of course, she had no idea why Dario—who, according to the few things she'd read about him on the internet, had never even given an interview to a tech journalist before now—would agree to something this intrusive. But, as usual, he'd deflected her questions the night before.

She hadn't pressed because she was already struggling with a severe case of sexual frustration, which had kept her awake every night for over a week—becoming more persistent after each evening she had to spend in his company. In the last ten days, since she'd arrived in Italy, she'd only had one night when Dario wasn't escorting her to some new event, or opening, or exclusive party. And annoyingly, that night had been worse than the others, because she'd actually missed the infuriating man. Which was preposterous, because they weren't in a real relationship.

There had been no repeat of his proposition in the limousine on the way to the opera. In fact, he had barely spoken to her on the rare occasions when they had been alone together since. He hadn't set foot inside her apartment since that first night, always waiting in the car now when collecting her. And she'd never visited his apartment, until now.

When they were together for the short drive to whatever event they needed to be 'seen' at, he kept the dividing screen down so the chauffeur could hear every word—almost as if he wanted to ensure nothing could happen between them. But once they stepped into the glare of the public spotlight, his fierce gaze, those possessive, provocative touches that he was a master of—his hand gripping her waist, his palm resting on her back, the light brush of his lips against her neck as he whispered something in her ear like a besotted lover—had begun to drive her insane.

Of course, his behaviour around her in public was all part of the subterfuge they had agreed to. But occasionally, she caught him watching her with that fierce desire in his eyes, and she knew he still wanted her… And unfortunately, whenever he stood too close, and she inhaled the intoxicating scent of sea salt and lemons from his cologne, or felt his gaze on her, she knew their 'chemistry' was still there. And getting worse. Because she wanted him too, desperately.

The thought of sitting through an interview with a journalist, though, filled her with dread. Not only had she never spoken to the press before, she wasn't sure why he had decided to include her. There were so many ways she could screw this up. But when she'd told him about her concerns in the car last night, Dario had simply shrugged and murmured, 'Do not concern yourself, it will be conducted mostly in Italian. All you need to do is look as if you want me.'

She sighed as Aldo led her through the huge penthouse apartment towards the living area. Well, at least *that* wouldn't be a struggle—after the dreams which had been waking her in the dark, hot and sweaty and desperate for those devastating touches in that darkened limo on their first date, which he had denied her since.

Dario stood when she entered the large open-plan living room. He looked tall and gorgeous in a pair of jeans and a black polo-neck sweater which clung to the impressive contours of his chest. Her heart stuttered, the familiar blush rising into her cheeks on cue. How could he be even more devastating in casual clothing than he was in a tux? How was that fair?

'*Ciao*, Tallulah,' he said, lifting her fingers to his lips, his gaze rivetted to her burning cheeks as he pressed his lips to her knuckles.

He introduced her to the journalist, an impeccably dressed older woman called Gianna Lombardi with a shrewd smile on her face. After congratulating them both on their recent engagement, Gianna placed a recording device on the coffee table between them while explaining how much her readers were looking forward to hearing the details of their whirlwind romance.

What details? She didn't have any details, because Dario hadn't briefed her for this interview.

Tali's nerves started to strangle her. Perhaps sensing her distress, Dario laid a steadying hand on her hip and directed her to sit beside him on the sofa. And suddenly it wasn't the prospect of the interview that made her heart reverberate in her chest, but the awareness of him, his arm placed casually across the back of the sofa behind her, the brush of his muscular denim-clad thigh against her bare leg boxing her in and the tantalising scent of citrus and man which engulfed her.

She swallowed, trying to focus on the journalist and look the part of a woman comfortable in her fiancé's presence, and disguise the fact her pulse had kicked up to warp speed and her nipples had begun to throb against her bra.

His fingers skimmed over her hair, and he leaned close to whisper in her ear. 'Relax, *tesoro*.'

Even though she knew his affectionate words were for the journalist's benefit, the husky tone had her giddy heartbeat sinking into her abdomen. She crossed her legs, trying to squeeze the brutal pulse of awareness between her thighs into submission, as the journalist watched them both like a raptor.

'Signora Whittaker is it true that you speak no Italian?' the journalist asked.

'Not much,' Tali replied, caught off guard by the random question. 'But I—I'm taking lessons,' she offered.

Dario's thigh tensed, and his fingers stilled on her hair.

The journalist let out a harsh laugh. 'You did not know this, Signor Lorenti?' the woman asked.

'Of course,' he lied smoothly. 'I suggested it and Tallulah is keen to learn.'

Tali glanced back at him. If he was surprised at the news, it was hard to tell, because his face had gone carefully blank. But his body language suggested he was nowhere near as relaxed as he had been when she'd arrived.

Had she made a mistake? So soon.

She hadn't told him about the lessons she'd arranged

through Aldo, because she hadn't thought he'd mind. In fact, she'd hoped he might even be pleased, when she had more than a few basic phrases to rely on… And the truth was she'd enjoyed taking the classes with her tutor, Maria. The app she'd been using had been great for learning vocabulary, but she wanted to learn to speak the language. Plus, it helped fill up the long hours each day after she'd finished her morning session going over all the day's business with Ellie at Westwick and checking in with her mum…and before the stylist and her team arrived in the afternoon to dress her for her next 'date' with Dario.

She'd always been active and busy, and there were only so many books she could read or long walks through the Brera she could go on. Plus, not being able to converse in Italian made her feel at even more of a disadvantage in Dario's world.

'I'm enjoying the lessons, it's a beautiful language,' she added when Dario remained ominously silent.

'This is good, yes,' the journalist said absently, but then her gaze shifted to Dario and sharpened. 'But, still, it is surprising you have fallen in love with a British woman, Signor Lorenti,' the woman said, still speaking in English, the shrewd smile becoming positively sly, the implied criticism of Dario's choice hard for anyone to miss.

'Why would this be a surprise?' Dario replied, his voice calm, but Tali could hear the frigid note of disapproval. His hand swept down her back, to settle on her hip, the intimate touch making her shiver. 'Tallulah is accomplished in many things, and exceptionally beautiful, what man could want more in a wife?'

The journalist's expression became flat and direct. 'And yet, you have never dated an Englishwoman before now.

Everyone assumed you would marry an Italian, given your estrangement from your British father, Lord Westwick.'

'My father has been dead for seven years, Signora Lombardi,' Dario shot back, as his hand tightened on Tali's hip, signalling his fury at the line of questioning. 'He has no bearing on my choices, now or ever,' he finished, but the sharp tone couldn't disguise the fact he hadn't denied what she'd said.

While Tallulah had always known about Dario's difficult relationship with his father—given the man's absence from his gravely injured son's bedside during most of that summer and the cruel way he had spoken to him the one time he had visited him—Dario's volatile reaction now felt revealing in a way she hadn't expected.

Was it true? Had he deliberately *avoided* dating British women?

That he didn't want to discuss his dating preferences, or his father though was obvious, but the journalist refused to take the hint. Her eyes gleamed, like a shark's while going in for the kill.

'And yet, it is said he refused to allow you to speak Italian as a boy, after your mother died. That must have been extremely hard, as according to my sources you spoke very little English. But now you will have to speak English again when you wish to converse with your wife?'

Dario sat upright, the relaxed demeanour history, and said something to the woman in rapid Italian. Tali only caught a few words, one of which was the Italian for 'stop'—*fermare*. But she didn't need to fully understand what he was saying to know he was no longer disguising his anger at the line of questioning, especially when the woman's face went red. And she looked visibly shaken.

'*Mi scuso*, Signor Lorenti,' she said, the obsequious

tone not doing much to reduce the tension snapping in the air. 'I am sorry, Signora Whittaker,' she added, sending Tali a strained smile, the smug look gone. 'Please accept my apologies.'

'Of course,' Tali replied, trying to smooth over the incident, and figure out what exactly the journalist was apologising for.

'We can continue,' Dario said, but the steel in his voice sounded anything but accommodating when he added, 'But questions about my father are not permitted.'

The rest of the interview was conducted in both Italian and English, the woman's fawning questions making it easy for Tali to stick to the story of their whirlwind romance without having to give the details she didn't have. But Dario's answers remained short, his tone curt, until Gianna mentioned Dario's sister, Mia, and the man she was due to marry—Sante Trovato—during a question in Italian. Tali thought it was an innocuous enquiry about Dario's intention to attend the wedding. At that point, though, his patience evaporated, and he cut the interview short.

The name Trovato sounded vaguely familiar to Tali. Was he one of Lorenti Corp's business rivals? Because Dario seemed almost as unhappy talking about his sister's groom as he had been discussing Lord Westwick.

As the journalist was shown out by Aldo, the woman looked a lot less confident than she had when Tali had first arrived. But as soon as the door to the salon closed behind her, Tali's shoulders sagged with relief. At least showtime was over.

Not that it had been a particularly successful showtime.

Dario strode to the apartment's elaborate terrazzo, his limp more pronounced than usual. Tali stood alone in the salon and watched him. Tension still bristled in the air. She could sense his displeasure in the stiff, unyielding stance, the silence which seemed to throb with anger. Whatever the interview was supposed to have achieved, it hadn't. She hoped she wasn't responsible for that…

She forced herself to swallow the questions she wanted to ask about Dario's impatient replies to the journalist's questions. His difficult relationship with Lord Westwick was none of her business, and neither was his apparent displeasure about the man his sister had chosen to marry. Although perhaps she'd misunderstood that. Because they were going to be attending the wedding. Surely, he would not have agreed to go to Sicily if he had some beef with Trovato?

'Well, that went well,' she murmured.

She turned to leave, feeling like an interloper, but as her heels clicked on the salon's polished wood flooring, a harsh demand echoed across the cavernous space.

'*Aspetta*, wait,' he said, his tone tight with frustration.

He walked towards her, his uneven gait doing nothing to slow his stride. But as his gaze locked on her face, her heartbeat throbbed into her throat.

Had she screwed up again? Because he did not look pleased. When he spoke, though, he said the last thing she had expected. 'There is no need for you to learn Italian, it is not part of our agreement.'

'I—I know,' she said. Why was he looking at her like that, as if she was a puzzle he could not solve?

His brows furrowed. 'Nor will ingratiating yourself with me increase my desire to invest in Westwick Hall.'

She flinched, the cutting remark like a physical blow.

While they had hardly become friends in the past week and a half—because he was even more unknowable now than he had been in Wiltshire—and the tormenting chemistry only added another layer of tension when they were together, which made it even harder to break down the barriers between them, she had believed he at least respected her.

Apparently, she'd been wrong.

The temper she'd been holding on to—during the hours she spent being dressed up like a mannequin, or whenever Aldo delivered another of Dario's demands without an explanation, or every time the hot pulse of awareness became unbearable while he toyed with her in public—exploded in her chest.

'Well, thanks, that's good to know!' she replied, each word dripping with sarcasm. 'You know, this gig would be a whole lot easier if you deigned to tell me what the hell you *actually* want, instead of treating me like an inconvenient accessory you have to pet in public but who you can't stand to even look at in private.'

That damned eyebrow rose, his expression still cynical, still unmoved.

'You know perfectly well why I will not touch you again in private,' he growled. 'Because it is torturous enough having to touch you in public. I have not had a good night's sleep for over a week.'

The edge in his voice, and the suggestion this was all her fault—*again*—had the last thin thread she had on her temper snapping in two.

'Oh, just shut up.' She took a breath, more than ready to let him have it with both barrels. 'You think you're the only one who can't sleep without imagining us together naked? News flash, you're not. And *you* were the one who started it,' she all but howled—not caring anymore if she sounded like a five-year-old having a temper tantrum. 'And FYI, it's not my fault that interview was a disaster, when you wouldn't even tell me what you wanted me to say to that woman. Or why you agreed to an interview in the first place when it's clearly not your happy place to be quizzed about your private life.'

'This marriage must appear real—so speaking to the press was necessary…' he replied, his jaw so tight now she was surprised he didn't crack a tooth. 'And FYI, *you* agreed to do this job. If you no longer want it, perhaps you should say so.'

'Uh-huh.' So, they were back to one of his bloody ultimatums, were they? She threw up her hands, having had enough of those, too. 'Well, FY *another* I, perhaps if you stopped behaving like an entitled arse and told me why you *need* this marriage, I wouldn't feel so out of my depth.'

She swung round, intending to storm out of the apartment, not caring anymore if he called a halt to the whole arrangement. She couldn't live under his constant disapproval any longer. Because it was not only driving her insane—it reminded her of that time in her life when she had felt rudderless and confused, desperate to understand why her father didn't love her the way he loved his other children, while being terrified of the possible answer to that question… That there was something intrinsically wrong with her, which made her less loveable, less worthy than them.

But before she had managed to go two paces, a hard hand clamped around her wrist.

'*Fermare!*' he said, as he hauled her around to face him. And suddenly she was inches from that hard chest, those vivid gold eyes glaring at her, but the expression in them was not anger, or condemnation…but the same furious, untamed hunger which had been torturing her for days.

'My father hated that I did not want his title, or his estate. So, he made it a requirement in his will that I marry an Englishwoman, to inherit the house he owned on Capri where I lived with my mother.' He said the words through gritted teeth. 'For seven years, I have tried to purchase Palazzo di Constanzo from my father's Trustees without succumbing to his blackmail. But I have invested a fortune in the property, and *still* they refuse to let me own it outright. *This* is why I need you as my wife...'

She shuddered, shocked he had confided in her, but even more shocked to see the shadow of hurt beneath the swirl of temper and fierce desire in those molten brown eyes. Because it reminded her of that surly, desperately unhappy teenager—injured and in pain—who had pushed her away so often that summer, like a wild animal caught in a trap.

The sense of connection, of shared pain, made her heart hammer her chest wall. The bite of temper disappeared until all she felt was compassion for the injured boy who still lurked inside the man. Maybe he really believed this marriage was about owning his mother's old home...and defying the man who had tried to keep it from him. But she doubted that was the whole story, however much he might want to believe it. Perhaps his desperation to own the palazzo was also a way of righting the wrongs his father had done to him. All those years ago. She knew how that felt, because she'd spent so long fantasising herself, about making her father regret discarding her, as well.

And to think she had convinced herself in the past two weeks that that boy had become a cold man, who felt nothing.

She pressed her palm to his scarred face, hoping to soothe, desperate to heal.

'Your father sounds like an even bigger prick than mine,' she managed. 'You deserved better, and so did I.'

The muscle in his cheek jumped and flexed against her palm, but then he flinched and let her go. Swearing under his breath, he walked back to the terrace.

He stood with his back to her, staring out at the late-afternoon sun. But his stance lacked the rigid control which had always intimidated her.

She followed him out onto the balcony. 'Is it true? What the journalist said? That he wouldn't allow you to speak Italian?' Maybe she had no right to ask, but suddenly she wanted to know exactly how bad it had been for him. Because while her father had chosen to be absent for much of her life, she had always had her mum. While Dario, it seemed, had had no one to protect him.

He shrugged, but the movement was far too stiff to be nonchalant. 'I do not require your pity,' he said, his tone brusque again.

She sighed. *So that would be a yes, then.*

'All I require is that you do the job I have asked of you,' he continued. 'And I did not ask you to learn Italian.'

Why was he so hung up on her decision to learn the language he obviously loved and preferred to use—especially if his father had used English as a means of punishment when he was a boy? It made no sense. But she forced herself to take a mental step back.

She'd always been too willing to believe the best of people, too desperate to want to heal anything and everything she thought might be wounded, or sad, or need her help. And she had the scars to prove it… All those nicks and scratches caused by the wild animals who had quite literally ended up biting the hand that had tried to feed them… Her mum had called it her Miss Fix-it complex.

Dario Lorenti wasn't that lonely boy now. He was a man who guarded his pain as vehemently as he guarded his privacy. And he'd made it very clear he didn't value her sympathy.

'Do you really want me to stop the lessons?' she asked, carefully.

She didn't want to give them up, for so many reasons—one of which was she didn't want him to resent having to speak to her in English… Which was so screwed up considering he was the one insisting she stop. But Dario was paying for the tutor Aldo had hired, so if he asked her to stop, she would have to.

He turned, and the perplexed frown on his face had the sympathy squeezing her ribs again. Did he even know why this was troubling him so much?

'I have said it is not necessary.'

'I know, but… I'm enjoying the lessons—they're a lot more fun than having to get prodded and poked by the stylist. And I wasn't lying when I told Mrs Lombardi I think it's a beautiful language. Plus, it would totally make our love affair look more convincing…' She shrugged, starting to become wary herself of how much she wanted to continue to learn Italian. 'If I'm making the effort to learn your language, you know…' She stumbled to a halt. Was she making too big a deal of this? Because the yearning to speak to him in his native tongue felt like more than just a way to pass the time. Was she trying to please him without realising it? And to what end, when they both knew this relationship wasn't real?

He stared at her for the longest time, but then his lips curved, the half smile more rueful than amused. He brushed his thumb across her cheek and tucked a lock of hair behind her ear.

She shivered, the automatic response something she couldn't control as the unrequited yearning flared back to life. It was the first time he had touched her when she was alone with him since their charged moment in the limo ten days ago.

'I can think of a much better way to make our love affair more convincing,' he murmured, the low tone reverberating in all her pulse points. The promise in his eyes was as potent and provocative as it had been ten days ago…and just as terrifying.

She pressed a palm to her own cheek, aware of the sizzle of sensation where his thumb had cruised across her skin. She wanted to sleep with him, wanted to find out where this terrifying chemistry would lead, but she felt even more exposed now than she had ten days ago, the tiny glimpse into his past bringing back the fierce sense of connection she'd always felt for that surly, unhappy boy.

She nodded. 'I want you, too,' she admitted, because there was no point in denying it, especially as she'd already broken cover during their argument.

'I know,' he said.

He cradled her face in warm palms, his gaze fixed on hers, and lowered his head to slant his lips across hers.

She sobbed, shocked by the blast of heat and longing, as her mouth moulded to his. He took his own sweet time, tempting, tormenting, swallowing her sighs, absorbing the shimmer of fear. His lips were persuasive, firm, demanding, his tongue even more so as it pressed into her mouth.

She opened for him, her breathing already ragged, her sex already aching, her breasts trapped against his chest as the kiss turned from subtle to scorching in a heartbeat.

His fingers threaded into her hair, angling her head to take more, to take all. His lips commanding, controlling, his tongue delving deep, over and over, exploring, and exploiting each sigh, each sob, each shudder.

She could feel herself falling into the sensual fog, the dazed, dizzying desire, too much and yet not enough.

One hand gripped her bottom, to drag her against the thick ridge in his jeans. Her core melted, as she writhed against it, needing more, but scared to take it, to demand it. Her emotions were still in turmoil from their argument. And that weird sense of connection which felt so real.

She pressed her hands against his chest and pushed him away, more confused and wary than ever, even though the sensations shimmering through her bloodstream still fired her need.

He released her. His breathing was as harsh as her own, his face set in hard lines—his eyes a molten gold.

'I'm… I'm sorry,' she said. 'I'm sending you mixed messages and I don't mean to…' she managed around the desire and panic making her throat feel raw.

Of course, he'd kissed her. She'd told him she wanted him.

But instead of reacting angrily to her rejection, as she had feared, he brushed his thumb across her cheek again, then pressed it to her lips.

'Do not apologise,' he said. 'Are you a virgin, Tallulah?'

Embarrassment scorched her cheeks, at the direct question—and the potent hunger in his gaze.

'No… No, I'm not,' she said.

'But you have little experience, am I correct?' he asked again, the rueful tilt of his lips making the blush explode.

'Well…yes, I suppose so, compared to you,' she answered. What did he expect her to say? And why was he looking at her with indulgence, even affection? Because it was making her feel a whole lot more exposed, while he seemed to be in complete control again.

He let out a rough chuckle. But when he cupped her

cheek there was no denying the fierce need in his expression, which matched her own. 'Then we must take this slowly. Because our passion is extraordinary…and I do not wish to hurt you.'

'Ummm, okay,' she said, pretty sure her cheeks were probably visible from outer space by now.

Pulling her closer, he pressed his lips to her burning forehead. 'You may continue with your Italian lessons.'

It took her a moment to figure out what he was talking about, her mind dazed from the endorphin high still powering through her system. 'Okay.'

'I will see you on Friday, for the trip to Sicily.'

She frowned. 'We don't have any other dates in Milan over the next two days?' she asked, pretty sure they were scheduled to attend an embassy party that evening, but her mind was still too fuzzy to remember the details.

Taking her hand, he led her towards the apartment's lift, then kissed her knuckles in that habitual gesture—which should have seemed perfunctory but made the heat rush through her all over again.

'I think it best we do not spend too much time alone together, until you are ready for more.'

'Okay,' she said again, like a dummy.

It wasn't until she'd stepped into the lift though and watched the doors close on him that it occurred to her the yearning in her sex had only got worse. She had agreed there would be more. Although she had no clue what 'more' entailed.

She rubbed her hand across her mouth, feeling the imprint of his lips on hers, the electrifying rasp of his stubble, the harsh demand of his tongue, the press of that huge erection against her belly. The mark of his ownership so much more elemental now than the diamond ring on her finger.

That the realisation was as exhilarating as it was terrifying only made the days ahead seem like more of a minefield… Because she had the sneaking suspicion that as well as having a lot less sexual experience than Dario Lorenti, she was also nowhere near as well versed at ruthlessly controlling her emotions.

CHAPTER EIGHT

Two days later

AS THE LORENTI CORP helicopter circled Sante Trovato's sprawling Palermo estate, the neoclassical grandeur of his home a testament to how high the former Sicilian slum kid had risen, Dario's stomach churned. He rubbed his leg, the muscle cramps triggered by brutal memories of that long-ago summer day when Sante had deserted him—the acrid scent of burnt rubber, the metallic taste of blood, the crushing weight on his thigh, the fear and pain spent drifting in and out of consciousness.

Tension screamed across his shoulder blades. He'd seen Trovato in passing over the years since that day. How could he have avoided the man, after the Sicilian had managed to turn his coding abilities—abilities which Dario had nurtured and encouraged when they were schoolboys together in that godforsaken boarding school in Wiltshire—into the sale of an app that had made him a billionaire several years before Lorenti Corp had begun to corner the European market in a similar field. Since then, Trovato's ambitions had known no bounds, but at least he wasn't heavily involved in the tech business anymore, preferring to invest in property.

Even so, Dario was livid about having to meet the man again and suffer his hospitality. What exactly was Trovato's game? Pretending to love Mia? Asking for her hand in marriage? There had to be an ulterior motive—because Sante Trovato never did anything without one. The man was a user, a betrayer. Dario had discovered that the hard way.

He heard Tallulah gasp through the headphones as the chopper coasted over the citrus and olive groves, the elegant architectural flourishes of fountains and guest houses from a bygone era, the glistening waters of a swimming pool surrounding by exotic blooms which blended in seamlessly with the ornate gardens… Heat eddied in his gut, triggered by his fake fiancée's reaction to Trovato's ostentatious home.

As if it wasn't bad enough he was having to attend this wedding on enemy turf—and quite possibly witness his sister marry a man he despised and who he had already told her she could never trust—he was having to do it while coping with the worst case of blue balls he had ever experienced.

What the hell had he been thinking, kissing Tallulah after that intrusive interview? It had been a mistake of epic proportions. He had slept even less in the nights since, and had to take himself in hand more than once—like a horny teenager instead of a man who could have any woman he desired… Except the one strapped into the helicopter beside him, pretending to be his fiancée—her eyes wide, her cheeks flushed, her breasts pressed enticingly against the soft fabric of the demure designer dress.

The irony did not escape him that when Gianna Lombardi's article had been published yesterday, it had been much more favourable to their cause than he had expected after the journalist's antagonistic questions about his father… Lombardi had declared their whirlwind romance a love for the ages, and Tallulah the woman who had tamed Milan's biggest playboy—mostly because of his unguarded reaction to the news his fake fiancée was learning Italian. The feature writer had been touched by his surprise, apparently. The truth was he had not been surprised, he had been shocked, not just by Tallulah's decision, but by his knee-jerk reaction to it… That fierce yearning to have his fake bride speak to him in his own language—the language his father had once punished him for using—had been swift and sudden, and reminded him of that confused, unhappy, desperately lonely boy. An emotional response he despised…

He glared out of the window, his confused reaction tormenting him all over again. Why should he care if she learned Italian, or what language she spoke to him in? Theirs was no more than a temporary arrangement. Surely that illogical response was simply a result of being unable to feed the hunger which had only got worse since that damn kiss. But instead of coming to him as he had expected—because he knew she yearned for him, too—she had remained wary and aloof.

He had planned to wait until she admitted she wanted to change the terms of their arrangement, too. Pressuring women was not his style, but when had he ever wanted one as much as he wanted her? It was lowering to realise he was starting to become obsessed with her, which was also not something he had ever experienced before either—because he had always known it made you weak to wish for something you did not have.

Now more than ever, he needed the release only good, hard, sweaty sex could give him, to navigate the days ahead. He was already wound too damn tight at the thought of seeing Trovato with his sister. But the prospect of having to treat Tallulah like a lover in public while being unable to touch her in private was an additional torment which threatened to make this trip even more unbearable.

The helicopter settled onto the heliport at the back of the palazzo, once the home of a Sicilian prince. After the blades had powered down, they were greeted by a small army of staff, who would collect their luggage and escort them to the main residence.

As they were led into a huge entrance hall and towards a wide, sweeping marble staircase—already decorated with local blooms and ribbons for the wedding that evening—the grinding pit of resentment in Dario's stomach grew.

He did not wish to be here, forced to socialise with his enemy. But he was doing this for Mia, in one last-ditch attempt to make her see reason.

As they ascended the staircase behind the staff member who had introduced himself as Trovato's *maggiordomo*, he pressed his palm to Tallulah's back.

'I wish to speak to my sister in private, once you have been introduced,' he murmured against her ear. 'Will you be okay alone for an hour?'

'Of course, the estate looks amazing. Maybe I could explore? Is the wedding due to take place tomorrow?' she asked, but the polite smile she sent him only increased his irritation. Why was she treating him like a stranger when the taste of her mouth, the memory of her sobs still tortured him?

'It is scheduled for tonight. It appears to be a fairly modest affair by Sicilian standards as it has been so rushed.' The haste was another warning sign, as far as Dario was concerned, of Trovato's dishonest intentions. 'I certainly do not intend to remain as Trovato's guest for more than one night…' he snapped. Assuming, of course, he could not persuade his sister to see the light and call off this farce at the eleventh hour. But knowing how impulsive and naïve Mia had always been—and how unwilling to accept his advice—he already suspected he was on a fool's mission.

'You're unhappy about the wedding?' Tallulah asked softly, the confusion in her eyes reminding him of her expression when he had questioned her decision to take Italian lessons. Why did that look get to him so much?

'No, I am not happy that my sister has chosen to marry that man,' he said, giving away more than he had intended. Very few people knew of his former connection with Trovato, and he wished it to remain that way. The man no longer had the power to hurt him. He had lived with the consequences of that day ever since, but in some ways, he welcomed the wounds which would never heal. They had made him stronger and more resilient—and would always remind him never to trust anyone the way he had once trusted Trovato.

Because the boy who was supposed to be his best friend had deserted him after the accident, when his father had offered Trovato money to disappear. Trovato had taken the bribe rather than remaining loyal to him. Dario had waited for days in the hospital, in pain, sure his friend would defy his father's version of events and come to see him… But he never had. And then Dario had known everything his father had said was true. Trovato had not gone to get help after the accident, he had run, and he had only befriended Dario in the first place because his father had money… Something Trovato had always yearned for.

He could see the questions in Tallulah's expressive face about his animosity towards his sister's choice of husband, but before she could ask any of them, the *maggiordomo* opened the door to a large drawing room, announced their arrival, and closed the door behind them to give them privacy.

He spotted his sister and Trovato standing together near an impressive fireplace, waiting to greet them. The room's expensive antique furniture and forbidding grandeur did nothing to dim the excitement and expectation on his sister's face. But as Dario's gaze landed on Trovato, the man tensed, and the weight in Dario's stomach twisted, the bitterness so sharp he could taste it.

They looked like a unit, with his sister positioned in front of Trovato. The Sicilian had his hand on Mia's shoulder—his stance both possessive and protective. As if Mia needed protecting from her own brother, instead of the man who was trying to exploit her.

The thought of the difficult conversation he had in his near future with Mia made resentment flare in his gut. Forcing him into this situation was just another of Trovato's betrayals—a way to drive a final wedge between Dario and the only family he had left.

His relationship with Mia had become increasingly difficult ever since they had left Capri and their once carefree childhoods behind. He knew part of that distance was his fault. He'd tried to look out for Mia. She'd been so young and much more vulnerable than him when their lives had been torn apart. And her passionate nature, her stubborn pride, her generous heart and her foolish lack of caution had left her open to exploitation. Her blank refusal to accept his financial help had only made matters worse—frustrating him and forcing her to seek employment with men like Trovato, who would exploit their connection.

But something about the way they stood so close together, the wary look in Trovato's eyes, pricked his memory. He sealed off the thought and gripped Tallulah's hand to walk towards them. Tallulah's telltale shiver of response to his touch felt strangely vindicating. Despite the frustrations their fake relationship had caused, he was grateful in that moment to have her by his side, because facing this bastard and his sister alone would somehow be harder.

'Dario…' Mia whispered, then left Trovato's side to rush to them both. *'Grazie mille, Dario, tu venuto!'* He could see the genuine pleasure to see him in her bright smile and the affection in her eyes as she greeted him.

'I said I would come,' he murmured, switching to English.

The unguarded happiness in her expression dimmed. And he had a sudden recollection of the puppy she'd once brought to Westwick Hall, on one of the rare occasions they'd spent the summer there. It was the summer he had brought Trovato home with him from boarding school because his friend had had nowhere else to go. Mia had adored that puppy and been desperate to keep the pet, but their father—when he arrived—had been furious to see the mongrel dog. Mia had been devastated when their father had the puppy taken from her and returned to the nearby farm where she'd found it.

Of course, Dario was the cause of her sadness today. But he forced himself not to acknowledge the prickle of guilt. Sentimentality would not help this situation. And he had always had Mia's best interests at heart, unlike their father, who had only ever cared about appearances. And unlike Trovato, who had shown his true colours by abandoning Dario to his fate after that accident. Trovato had taken their father's blood money after the crash and used it to build an empire. And now he intended to take Dario's sister from him, too.

To hell with that.

'This must be your fiancée,' Mia declared, the too bright smile back as she turned to Tallulah, no doubt desperate to break the tension between Dario and her fiancé. Reaching out, she grasped Tallulah's free hand, the warmth in her expression making Tallulah's blush brighten. 'It's so wonderful to meet you, Tallulah. I read all about your whirlwind affair with my brother this morning in *Ragazza* magazine. About how you are the beauty who has tamed the playboy… This is indeed a feat.' His sister's delighted laugh pricked at Dario's conscience. He would have mentioned to his sister his marriage was a stunt to gain ownership of their mother's palazzo, but given she was now firmly under Trovato's spell, he could no longer trust her.

'Thank you, I think,' Tallulah said with an uncomfortable laugh, her surprise at Mia's enthusiasm visible when she glanced at Dario.

He cleared his throat, determined to ignore that look, which seemed to be questioning why he had not told Mia the truth. He had explained to his fake bride why he needed this marriage—against his better judgement. His relationship with his sister, and what he chose to confide in her, was certainly no concern of Tallulah's.

'When is your wedding going to be?' Mia asked, apparently oblivious to the subtext. 'I hope Sante and I will be able to attend,' she offered, the olive branch hard to ignore.

But the mention of his ex-friend's first name—a name he had not used to refer to the man, even in his own head, since that summer—had Dario's fury and frustration returning.

'I am not here to discuss my wedding, Mia. But yours. We must speak, alone.'

Mia flinched at his harsh tone, her face falling. He saw

the hurt in her eyes, so like their mother's, but when she spoke, he could also hear steel.

'If you've come here to browbeat me into calling off my wedding to the man I love, Dario,' his sister said, switching into Italian, he suspected to save Tallulah any more discomfort, 'you've made a wasted journey.'

It occurred to him in that moment that while he'd always felt his sister had the same flaws as their mother, he could see in her stubborn expression she had an emotional strength their mother had lacked. But right now, he was finding it impossible to appreciate the revelation—because this foolhardy decision was so misguided.

But then Trovato stepped forward and placed that damn possessive hand back on his sister's shoulder. And it took every ounce of Dario's control not to punch the bastard.

'We need to talk, Dario, all three of us,' he said, also in Italian. 'Because there are many things I should have told you a long time ago. I let my pride get in the way—I refused to defend myself when you believed the worst of me. But I can see now my silence was as much to blame as your gullibility. I should never have let your father's lies about me fester between us all these years.'

Dario's temper sharpened, the words like a slap. The old anger, that miserable sense of betrayal, of being used and then discarded, had the old pain tearing through his insides.

'*My* gullibility?' he snapped. 'You left me on the side of the road to rot and took my father's money. *Bastardo*.' He released Tallulah's hand to pull his clenched fist back. But as he drove it forward, Trovato leaned back, making him punch air. His bad leg buckled, and he stumbled to the ground. Agonising pain shot through his knee and thigh, but the humiliation was worse. He could hear Tallulah's shocked cry, hear his sister's agonised attempts to calm him down. But it was Sante who grabbed him and helped him back onto his feet.

The fury engulfed him, but Sante's arms closed around his shoulders from behind, making it impossible to wrestle free of the bastard and land the punch. The pain in his injured leg spread to his lungs, making it hurt to draw breath, as something brutal rose up his chest, more agonising even than the cramping pain firing across his kneecap. It was as if he were suffocating again, pinned down as he had been for so long that day in the wreckage, terrified and alone and broken.

'Listen to me, Dario,' Sante huffed against his neck, his arms banded tight around Dario's chest, holding him up, holding him close. 'I love your sister with all my heart. This isn't a trick. She is everything I am not. You must let go of the hate. *He* did this to us, because he could. Don't let him win. Not again.'

Dario continued the struggle, but Sante was stronger, not having to battle the pain. His certainty, his compassion were somehow weakening Dario even more than his useless leg.

Suddenly he couldn't hold on to the hurt, the fury anymore, when all he felt was hollowed out. Exhausted.

'I didn't take his money, Dario. Not a cent. And I did not leave you, I went to get help.'

His sister stood before him then, her trembling hands pressing against his cheeks, robbing him of breath, making his throat tighten, his ribs hurt.

'It's true Dario, I saw the terrible wounds on his feet that day. He walked for miles but couldn't flag down a single car. He went to the hospital that night. He was desperate to see you. But our father had told the hospital staff not to let him in.' Tears welled in her eyes, and he felt them leaking into his heart like acid. 'Our father *wanted* to destroy your friendship. Can't you see, Dario? He wanted you to hate Sante, because *he* hated him, a poor Sicilian, a bad influence on his son and heir. He isolated you deliberately that summer.'

The last of his energy seemed to leach away, the words jumbling in his head, but making a horrible, hideous kind of sense as he recalled how his father had referred to Sante as 'the Sicilian guttersnipe.'

The cruel memories of his father's scorn for the boy he'd made his friend came flooding back. Memories he'd pushed to one side during the long, endless days in pain that summer with only the housekeeper's pity and her young daughter—and his own misery—to keep him company.

It felt as if everything were collapsing around him and reshaping itself into something he didn't recognise.

Dio, were they telling him the truth? How could they not be, when he had always known his father hated his Italian heritage, and the bastard had never made any secret of the fact he despised Dario's friendship with Sante, the poor scholarship kid.

He felt his shoulders droop, the exhaustion consuming him, destroying him all over again.

'Let me go,' he murmured.

Sante released him immediately. But when Dario turned, he saw the earnestness, the emotion in his friend's gaze. And all the things he had once loved about that boy—his intelligence, his ambition, his bravery, his fierce loyalty to his country, to his roots, to Dario—came back in a rush of memory so brutal it left him breathless.

Dario stared at the silk rug at his feet, the pain in his leg now nothing compared to the agony in his heart.

All this time, he had believed his father's lies. The lies of a man he knew had never loved him. *Why?* Because somehow it had been easier to have someone to blame for his pain…

Sante was right, he'd been a gullible fool.

'Please believe us, Dario,' Mia said again, the tears streaming down her face now.

He nodded, lifting his head to stare blindly at the lavish frescoes which decorated the room's walls and had been so lovingly restored. Finally, he forced his gaze back to his sister and the man he had once loved as a brother.

'I do…' His voice broke on the words, shaming him even more. But then he caught sight of Tallulah, over Mia's shoulder—all the colour had drained from her face. She could not possibly have understood what was being said. Not only had the whole conversation been conducted in Italian, but no one knew of his feud with Sante except the three of them. The pity in her eyes, though, made it clear she knew…somehow…she *knew* that he had been in the wrong here.

The shame blindsided him, that she had witnessed the terrible mess he had made of his only real friendship. It upset him even more, though, that he had never even slept with this woman and yet somehow her opinion mattered.

The nausea rolled through him. He thrust his fingers through his hair and buttoned his jacket, which had come undone during the struggle. Buying time, desperate to control the emotions he did not want to feel.

At last, he made his gaze connect with Mia's, but he couldn't make himself look at Sante. He owed the man an apology, for believing the lies his father had told him all those years ago. For letting them fester and grow all this time. Sante had tried to take some of the blame for that, but it was on him, and only him. Mia had tried to tell him all this on the phone weeks ago, and he hadn't listened. Because he hadn't wanted to.

Even so, the words he needed to say to Sante wouldn't come, so he forced himself to say the next best thing.

'If you wish, I will give you away tonight,' he said to Mia in English.

His sister's face brightened like the sun. 'Dario, yes, yes, that would mean so much to me.' She glanced at Sante, who seemed taken aback by the offer. 'To us both.'

She lifted on tiptoes and planted a kiss on his scarred cheek, and the scent he recognised from so long ago—when they had been happy together, as children on Capri, when everything had been so simple—crucified him. Somehow it disgusted him even more that he had been forgiven so easily.

How had he let them get so far apart? But how could he allow that closeness back, when it made him feel so weak?

'I love you, Dario,' Mia said softly. 'It feels good to finally have my brother back…'

He gave a stiff nod. 'I should wash up,' he said, desperate for an excuse to get away from the raw emotions battering him.

'We have put you two together in the summer house. It is secluded and intimate and charming,' Mia said, her words bubbling out, her emotions clearly as close to the surface as his own. 'You have three hours before the wedding. Would you like me to show you the way? And arrange for refreshments for you both?'

'We have already eaten.' He cut off her offer, not sure he could bear to spend a minute longer in her company—or

Sante's—contemplating how badly he had fucked up. 'Is it the place on the other side of the orange grove?' he asked stiffly, vaguely remembering the structure from when the chopper had landed, what felt like several lifetimes ago.

'Yes, yes,' Mia said. 'You should let me show you both to…'

'Mia, it's okay. I believe Dario needs some time alone with his fiancée,' Sante announced.

Dario's gaze connected with the man he had once considered his best friend. His only friend, really. He wasn't sure he had it in him to repair the friendship they had lost, wasn't convinced he even wanted to. But he could be grateful the man knew him well enough to understand he needed some time to figure out what to do to quell the emotions making his chest hurt.

But when Sante strode out of the room and appeared with his *maggiordomo*, directing the older man to show him *and* Tallulah to their accommodation, the vice clamped around his chest. Right alongside it, though, was the furious surge of lust as his fake fiancée grasped his hand and squeezed his numb fingers as if trying to reassure him.

He flinched, her pity only making him more disgusted with himself and his loss of control.

The rest of the day was going to be even more torturous if she attempted to talk to him about any of this. He had no desire to confide in her, in anyone—which meant he could not slake this damn lust now. It would have been so simple and uncomplicated to use their chemistry as a means of forgetting all this. But how could he, when his emotions were so unsettled?

But once they were shown into the summer house, she seemed to sense his withdrawal, because she murmured, 'I think I'll go for a run, if you…if you want some alone time.'

He blinked back the sudden urge to ask her not to leave him, shocking him to his core.

But then she murmured, 'Or I could stay? And we could talk.'

He tensed and forced himself to shake his head—despising the moment of weakness but hating even more that she had somehow seen it.

'*Talk?*' he murmured. 'The last damn thing I wish to do with you right now is talk, Tallulah,' he said.

She nodded, the blush blazing across her cheeks a vindication of sorts. 'Right,' she said, then jerked her thumb over her shoulder. 'I'll go for that run, then.'

She dashed off—treating him as if he were an unexploded bomb which she needed to be careful not to trigger. Her reaction would have been ironic, if it didn't make him feel so damn pathetic. What the hell had happened to the man who had always prided himself on being able to control his emotions?

What was far worse though, was that after she had changed into some athletic gear in the house's lavish bathroom, then left him to shower alone…he *felt* like an unexploded bomb. Because the hatred he had fostered for so long towards Sante, even his superior attitude towards his sister's reckless, overemotional behaviour, was no longer there to bolster his sense of self or make him proud of the man he had worked so hard to become. Instead, he felt adrift, in a sea of emotions he could no longer rely on—ashamed that even for a moment he had needed the support of a woman he had paid to pretend to love him.

Desperate to ignore the still throbbing pain in his leg and the brutal recollection of the scene with Sante and Mia, which kept playing on a loop in his head, and his pathetic reaction to the sympathy in Tallulah's eyes when she had offered to *talk* about it, he pressed a hand to the shower's glass tiles and imagined his fake fiancée instead, in the summer house's lavish—and only—bed.

His cock hardened, as he conjured images of her lush body lying naked on the linen sheets, her soft hair fanned out across the pillows, her eyes dark with lust, her turgid nipples begging for his lips, her evocative scent intoxicating his senses—as if she was all his. And *only* his. He grunted as the need crested, and the climax powered from his aching body to splatter against the tiles. The sickening shame returned, though, as he watched his seed wash away.

Damn it, masturbating would never be enough to quell this insistent hunger. Or help him to forget the terrible mistakes he'd made with Sante, and with his sister—and the shame of needing more from his stunt bride than he should, if only for a moment.

As he dressed in the tuxedo his staff must have packed—which he'd never actually considered he would have to wear—he contemplated the prospect of finally getting Tallulah to himself, later tonight. And realised the best way to diffuse this damn bomb had been obvious from the start.

He didn't *need* Tallulah, he merely wanted her, and not taking her had left him on edge this afternoon, magnifying his volatile reaction to Sante and Mia's revelations.

Tallulah was not a part of his past, nor could she ever be part of his future—so any complications sex would add to their fake relationship, and there would be a few, could be managed… And right now, those complications would be worth it if having her meant he could finally satisfy this all-consuming hunger, and control these brutal, untethered emotions once and for all.

* * *

Tali rounded the corner of the orchard garden, making her way back towards the summer house…and Dario. It was less than two hours now before Mia's wedding was due to take place. And the stylist and her team would be waiting for her. For once she didn't mind the thought of being 'dressed,' because she really didn't think she could be alone with Dario—not without offering him the sympathy and support he had already made it very clear he didn't want.

But how could she not feel compassion for him after witnessing his reaction to the altercation with his sister's fiancé?

His stance had been rigid with control as they'd been led to the summer house. But when she'd watched him fall to his knees during the fight, the pain which had ripped through his features had been nothing to the agonised expression moments later, when Trovato and then Mia had explained something to him in Italian—which had been too fast for her to understand.

She stopped at the water fountain to scoop a handful of water onto her neck. She'd run for over an hour through the estate—the acres of rolling vines, the groves of orange and lemon trees and the beautifully maintained gardens near the majestic house—unnoticed by the staff rushing to finish setting up the trestle tables in the garden to host the wedding feast. She'd always loved to run when she had a particularly thorny problem to decipher. And was there any problem thornier than her relationship with Dario Lorenti?

She hadn't understood what the passionate argument had been about—her Italian was hardly fluent. But she had been able to make an educated guess that Dario and

Trovato had a history which was a great deal more complicated than a simple business rivalry.

But even though she hadn't been sure of the context, seeing the emotions Dario had been unable to mask—sensing how broken he'd been after that confrontation and how alone he'd seemed when they'd got to the summer house—had made the sense of connection she'd been trying to deny that much stronger. Scarily stronger, when you factored in the kiss in his apartment in Milan forty-eight hours ago, which she also couldn't forget.

She sluiced her face with the cool water.

Whatever the deal is with Sante is not your business, Tali.

And trying to make it her business would be a mistake. Because Dario had already made it clear he was only interested in one thing from her.

And having to behave like Dario's devoted fiancée this evening—while knowing there was only one bed in that stunning summer house—was going to make dealing with him tonight hard enough.

Tali made her way along the path to the back of the house, so she could get to the summer house without being spotted by any of the guests who were already arriving on the lavish driveway at the front entrance. But as she went past the outbuildings, she spotted Mia, dressed casually in jean shorts and a T-shirt, chatting to one of her wait staff setting up for the feast that evening.

Tali paused, about to find another way back—because how awkward was it that Dario hadn't mentioned to his sister their so-called 'love for the ages' was a lie—when Mia spotted her and waved.

'Tallulah! Wait, I wanted to talk to you.'

Before Tali could make a dignified retreat or think up

an excuse to run, the bride had excused herself and was jogging towards her.

'Hi,' Tali murmured, her already sweaty face probably purple when Mia reached her. 'I… I should head back.' She pointed over her shoulder, the awkward going all the way to eleven. 'I expect the stylist will be waiting for me… and you probably need to get dressed, too.'

'Ha, yes. I'm going to be late, but I had to let Bianca know about a last-minute change to the seating plan… It's the EA in me. I can't help over-organising every detail.' The woman beamed the same sweet, generous smile which had made Tali feel so guilty when they'd been introduced. 'But luckily, it's the bride's prerogative to be late,' she added. 'And Sante is far too used to having me at his beck and call. Now, *finally*, I will get a chance to make *him* wait, which I intend to take full advantage of…' She laughed, her face lighting up at the mention of her groom. Tali's heartbeat slowed at the glow which suffused Mia's features. What must it be like, to know you had found your soulmate? Because from the words Tali had managed to decipher—and the expression on Sante Trovato's face when he had spoken about Mia to Dario during their altercation—that was one thing she had been sure of. The man adored Mia, and Mia adored him right back.

Tali let out a strained chuckle. 'That sounds like a plan…'

'But first…' Mia began, her expression sobering. 'I wanted to apologise for what happened earlier. I hope we didn't make you too uncomfortable?' she continued, looking genuinely concerned. The trickle of guilt became a flood. 'We're so glad you're here with Dario. And I'm so, *so* happy he's found someone who cares about him and wants to support him. He's been alone for so long…' Mia rushed ahead, but the earnest expression only made Tali feel worse about their deception.

Why hadn't he confided in his sister? While it was obvious Dario had been furious with her decision to marry Trovato, none of that was true anymore, was it? Perhaps Dario would tell her tonight?

'I'm sure Dario told you all about Sante, about the things he thought he had done to him—leaving him in the wreckage of that car… But none of that was ever true. And while I'm glad Dario finally knows those lies were all just another way our father tried to manipulate him, it must have been awkward for you to have to witness all that.'

You have no idea.

Tali bit into her lip, the guilt starting to make her feel as if she'd swallowed a rock. This conversation had gone way beyond awkward to just plain awful.

'I just… I want you to know I understand that,' Mia added. 'And if you have any reservations at all, about the truth of what really happened that day, I'd be happy to explain it all to you, in English. Because I'm sure you probably didn't understand a lot of what was being said and knowing my brother. Well…' Mia gave a hefty sigh, but then a rueful smile appeared. 'I very much doubt he has explained any of it to you—because he'd rather cut out his tongue than share and discuss, as I'm sure you're already well aware.'

Tali couldn't help the small smile that curved her lips, because the truth was, even though she wasn't Dario's *real* fiancée, she *did* know exactly how much he disliked sharing anything—his motivations, his secrets and his feelings most of all.

But then Mia launched into an explanation of the poor

Sicilian boy who had been Dario's only friend at boarding school in the UK…

And understanding dawned.

So Sante Trovato, the man Mia was about to marry, was the same boy her mother and the rest of the staff had whispered about at Westwick that summer. The boy who had supposedly left Dario on the roadside to die…except he hadn't.

The greasy knot in Tali's stomach became a snake, threatening to gag her as Mia's impassioned explanations continued. And Tali's avid curiosity about Dario's past only ramped up her guilt. She shouldn't be listening to any of this. He wouldn't want her to know… That much had been obvious from the closed-off expression on his face when she'd offered to discuss it with him at the summer house.

'Please, Mia… You have to stop talking!' she finally blurted out.

Mia stopped abruptly. 'What, why?' she asked, utterly confused.

'Because… I'm not… I'm just… Not…' Tali stumbled to a halt, the confession dying on her lips.

She was breaking a confidence, not to mention a binding NDA agreement, by telling Mia the truth about her arrangement with Mia's brother.

'It's okay, Tallulah, whatever it is, you can tell me…' Mia said, confusion giving way to compassion. And suddenly Tali understood. She couldn't lie about this. Even if Dario ended up suing her. Or pulling out of their agreement. She'd never intended for anyone to get hurt. And Mia would be hurt, if she continued to believe Tali *meant* something to Dario, that one day soon Tali would be a genuine part of their family. Mia was so obviously a good person—a kind, sweet, passionately loyal person—who wanted the best for her brother, even though it sounded as if he'd been as distant with her as he had with everyone else… And while a part of Tali desperately wanted to know *why* Dario found it so hard to let anyone in, even his own sister, she couldn't let Mia confide in her. Because Mia would regret it when she learned the truth. That Tali meant nothing to Dario, even if he was starting to mean something to her—which was probably just her delusional Miss Fix-it issues resurfacing.

'I'm not Dario's real fiancée. We're not in love. I only met him a couple of weeks ago…' The truth burst out.

Mia stared at her, her expression going from confused to completely dumbfounded. 'You're not getting married?'

'Well, yes, but… That's not real either. Well, it will be a real marriage, as in a legal one, but I won't be his real wife. He needed to marry an Englishwoman, to inherit his mother's… *Your* mother's palazzo in Capri. Something about the terms of your father's will. I guess the palazzo means a lot to him. Obviously.'

For goodness' sake, stop talking now... You sound like an imbecile.

Mia's eyes narrowed as the truth dawned on her, but the compassion remained. There was no anger, not even irritation in her tone when she spoke again. 'My brother is pretending to love you, so he can inherit Palazzo di Constanzo?'

'Well…yes,' Tali murmured. God, how had she not realised until this moment how crass and manipulative their arrangement sounded?

'And how did he persuade you to do this?' Mia asked, her tone still level, but the spike of irritation there, underneath. Weirdly, though, it did not seem to be aimed at Tali.

'I'm the estate manager at Westwick Hall… I love my

job, and the Hall, but it's been in decline for years, and since Dario inherited it, he hasn't wanted to have anything to do with it. He finally came to the estate a few weeks ago to inform me he was demolishing it… But then he agreed to invest two million euros in Westwick, which would secure its future and all our jobs…if I agreed to pose as… his…' Embarrassment gave way to shame as the truth got locked in her throat. 'To pose as his…'

'Shhh, it's okay, Tallulah.' Mia reached out and took Tali's hand, squeezing her fingers. Until that moment, she hadn't realised she was shaking. 'You haven't done anything wrong…'

Except she had. She'd lied to Mia, to Sante, to all the staff at Westwick. She'd even tried to lie to her mother…

Gripping Tali's hand, Mia pulled her to the fountain and encouraged her to sit on the low wall that surrounded it. Tali dropped onto the warm stone, stupidly grateful, because her legs were shaky now, too.

Mia sat down beside her, still holding her hand. The chirps of birds, the buzz of bees, the tinkle of the fountain, the distant rumble of cars as the guests arrived and the hum of activity from the staff nearby faded, until all Tali could hear was the hard thuds of her own heartbeat—telling her what an idiot she'd been.

'Tallulah, is my brother sleeping with you?' Mia asked gently.

'No,' Tali replied. 'God, no!' Because that would make this situation even more sordid. But the rush of heat quickening Tali's heartbeat and flame-grilling her cheeks had Mia's gaze sharpening.

'But he wants to? Am I right? That much is obvious from the way he looks at you, the way he touches you,'

Mia said with such confidence, the burning in Tali's cheeks got worse.

'That's all for show,' Tali managed, dying a little more inside. Because she knew it wasn't for show as far as she was concerned. And she had one devastating kiss that she couldn't forget, a whole lot of sleepless nights—not to mention the wettest wet dreams known to woman—to prove it.

'I hate to break it to you, Tallulah,' Mia muttered, 'but my brother is not that good an actor. If he was, he would not have fallen foul of our father so often—and been punished so harshly.'

Harshly how? Tali wanted to ask but stifled the urge—after all, her curiosity about Dario had only made this conversation more difficult.

'And we also have that gushing article in *Ragazza* as exhibit B,' Mia continued. 'Gianna Lombardi is a very shrewd journalist. She would not have been fooled that yours was a love match if some of what she saw wasn't real.'

'Well, he definitely doesn't love me,' Tali said, feeling oddly deflated. 'We hardly know each other. And he's made it quite clear he doesn't want to get to know me better.'

'But he does want to sleep with you. Tallulah,' Mia reiterated. It wasn't a question.

'Please call me Tali,' she replied. Because really, if she was going to have the most excruciating conversation of her entire life with this woman, it seemed only fitting Mia should address her by the name everyone knew her by, except Dario. 'And in the interests of full disclosure, I want to sleep with him, too,' she blurted out, because it seemed unfair to let Dario take all the blame. After all, she *had* kissed him back two days ago. And if he'd put any real moves on her since, she wasn't sure she would have been able to resist him. Her cheeks became radioactive. 'He's, well… He's very charismatic…' *And beyond hot.* But no way was she about to mention that to his sister. 'And, sometimes, I feel what he really needs is a friend. Which is silly, I know. But I always had a bad habit as a kid of taking in wounded creatures. And Dario seems… well, wounded too, I guess.'

Mia blinked, her expression changing, until a pensive smile brightened her features. 'You have feelings for my brother…'

Again, it wasn't a question, but Tali found herself nodding. What was it about this woman that made it so hard to lie to her?

'I guess I do. Which is nuts… I've known him for precisely two weeks, and he hasn't exactly been easy to deal with. But he fascinates me. He wants to appear cold and in control all the time, but I really don't think that's who he is… But how could I possibly know that? I'm sure it's just a delusion brought about by the sexual tension incinerating my brain cells.' It was Tali's turn to start babbling.

'Except it is *not* your brain which makes these decisions, Tali,' Mia said softly. 'It is your heart. And you are right about my brother…' she added.

'I—I am?' Tali asked.

'Yes,' Mia said, with complete certainty.

And for the first time since Tali had offered to stay with Dario, and he had shut her out, she felt less vulnerable, less insecure. 'How am I right?' Tali pressed, needing to know now if there was really more to the connection she had begun to sense with Dario, or if it had all been in her own head.

'You are right that he is not as cold or controlled as he

wants to pretend,' Mia said gently. 'When we were children in Capri, he always protected me. Our mother was beautiful and wild. She loved us, but she did not know how to look after us. When we came to England, our father tried to force all the wildness out of Dario. But to do that, he had to also force out all the joy. And he succeeded, when he turned Dario against Sante. The accident, and the way it crushed Dario's spirit, even more than his body, did the rest. But you are the first person I know who has seen the boy he once was, beneath the surface of that unhappy man. And only in a few weeks. Perhaps…' Mia paused. 'Perhaps if you give in to the desire you both feel, you might discover more of that boy?'

Tali's heart lifted, and the fierce desire surged… But she wasn't sure anymore if it was the hunger which had tormented her for weeks demanding to be satisfied, or the yearning to make that lonely, bedridden boy smile which was driving her desire to know Dario better now.

The only thing she did know was that she wasn't convinced she could resist it any longer.

'Signora Lorenti...' A young woman shouted across the courtyard, then rushed towards them, looking flustered. 'You must come. Signora Chiara is concerned there will not be enough time to get your hair styled.'

Mia jumped up and replied in Italian, looking flustered, too, but also incandescently happy, her excitement giving her face a golden glow in the dying sunlight. But before she could follow the young assistant to prepare for her wedding, she turned back to Tali.

'Do not give up on my brother, Tali. He has always needed someone who won't put up with his bullshit… And, although I do not like to think about my brother this way, if nothing else, good sex can be its own reward.'

Before Tali could reply, her unruly heart bobbing into her throat, Mia had disappeared into the palazzo.

But as Tali walked back, through the outdoor kitchen, past trays of delicious hors d'oeuvres being laid out on silver platters, her mind kept snagging on all the things Mia had told her about Dario and his past…

Surely, Mia's input proved one thing at least—that there *was* a fascinatingly complex man lurking behind the façade of the ruthlessly controlled autocrat.

Would it really be so wrong to try to find that man? Especially now she had finally admitted to herself, as well as Mia, she was tired of fighting the hunger which had tormented them both ever since that damn kiss.

CHAPTER NINE

DARIO STOOD AT the edge of the festivities, watching his sister dance with her new husband in the moonlight. The wine had flowed after the ceremony, during the banquet of local delicacies served on white linen and gold-rimmed plates in the open air. And now the two hundred guests were partying into the night, enjoying the fragrant air, redolent with the scent of orange blossom and jasmine.

He'd expected a more formal and extravagant event for a man of Sante's wealth and status, but Mia's influence had been everywhere—her energy, her passion and her lust for life—in all those thoughtful, personalised touches which had made her wedding so relaxed and enjoyable.

For everyone but him…

He'd walked her down the aisle of flowers and fairy lights in the orchard, as he'd promised, aware of his halting steps beside hers and the delighted smile on her face which made him feel like a fraud.

When she'd leapt into Sante's arms after they'd declared their vows, he couldn't quite control the stab of bitterness which remained—towards his old friend. Not because he still believed what his father had told him all those years ago, but because that anger, that resentment had helped sustain him for so long. And now, he felt hollow inside, without the familiar anger to keep the knowledge there was something fundamental missing from his life at bay.

Mia had included many familiar Capresi delicacies in her wedding feast. And watching her dance, getting into the groove of an old disco hit in her flowing ivory silk gown while Sante twirled her in his arms, reminded him of their mother—always wild, always beautiful, but unlike Mia, always searching for a high which had eluded her.

'She looks stunning, and so happy,' Tallulah whispered beside him.

He turned to find her watching him, her blue eyes shiny with emotion—no doubt seeing things he did not wish her to see.

Lust charged through his system though, when his gaze raked over her figure. The satin gown matched the deep turquoise of her irises, its simple lines clinging to her curves, the peaks of her breasts pressing against the fabric. His mouth watered, as the familiar hunger speared into his gut.

What was he waiting for? When giving in to this devastating chemistry would be the perfect way to forget all these pointless memories that were reminding him of the boy he'd once been—naïve and scared because so much of his life was outside his control—and not the man he had worked so hard to become, immune to the flaws that had once made his mother so weak.

Clasping her hip, he tugged her towards him and leaned down to press his lips to her neck. Her vicious shudder was a seductive payback as he whispered in her ear.

'You are stunning too, Tallulah.'

She stiffened, the flare of desire in her transparent expression like a flaming wand igniting his already volatile senses. But when he bit softly into her earlobe, then traced the delicate shell with his tongue, she planted her palms against the cotton of his shirt and gave him a gentle shove.

Her wide-eyed gaze searched his face, the familiar blush turning her pale skin to a burning red.

'Dario, please don't,' she whispered, for his ears alone. 'I know we have to put on a show, but all this play-acting is… It's making it hard for me to tell what's real and what's…'

He pressed his finger to her lips to silence her—strangely touched by her panicked request.

'I am not acting, Tallulah.' He banded his arms around her, to bring her flush against him, until her eyes widened even more—as her belly cradled the hard ridge of his growing erection. 'We must change the terms of our agreement.'

She blinked, the sheen of compassion and understanding in her eyes something he knew he should reject, but he was too desperate to have her to even care about that anymore.

The resentment, the loneliness, the sense he was standing on the edge of a boiling vat of despair and would tumble into if he could not get back his usual control… He wanted all these wayward emotions to fuck off. And the only way to do it was to bury himself inside her at last.

'How?' she whispered.

Was she being coy? Angling for a better offer? His cynicism wanted to believe it, but somehow, he knew that was not who she was.

He forced himself to release her, made himself button his tux jacket over the strident evidence of his desire, aware of the people around them. While the other guests were probably too drunk, and too high on the joy of his sister's wedding, to notice him and Tallulah, he did not wish to continue this conversation in public.

They needed to be alone. Because whatever happened next would not be for show—and was not for anyone's benefit but their own.

'Come.' He clasped her hand, to lead her past the throngs of people clapping and cheering as Sante swung his new wife into a romantic dip. Dario barely glanced their way though, all his focus on the woman whose fingers were clutched in his. 'Let us return to the summer house.'

'But what about your sister and Sante? Shouldn't we say goodbye?' she said, her voice trembling. 'Before they leave on their honeymoon?'

He led her to the edge of the gardens, aware of the summer house on the other side of the citrus orchard, its lights like a beacon as the night closed in.

'It is not necessary, I spoke to them both during the feast,' he said, the tension in his gut building at the recollection of the awkward conversation. He had formally apologised to his old friend, but the distance between them had remained. He'd made sure of it. He could not go back. Whatever lies had been exposed, he would never feel comfortable having the level of trust he had once had in Sante with anyone again. His sister had watched him with a peculiar expression on her face… Not quite pity, but not quite anything else either—which had only made the conversation more excruciating.

But he had done the right thing. And now he wished to forget the events of today, tonight. To live in the moment… and finally feed this driving hunger.

At last, they reached the summer house, the night drawing in around them. He hauled Tallulah through the door, slamming it shut to close off the faint sounds of the festivities from the other side of the estate. He released her, to take off his jacket, and tear off the tie which was starting to strangle him.

His mouth had dried. His breathing was now ragged.

She stood, shivering, despite the warmth of the evening, her breath heaving, too.

He let his gaze coast over that damn gown again, the shimmering satin accentuating the fullness of her breasts. While it was more demure than the gown he had objected to over two weeks ago in Milan, it had the same devastating effect. He'd wanted to rip it off her the minute she had walked out of the dressing room earlier—and been ready to murder every man whose gaze had lingered on her during the wedding.

Surely that was why he felt so on edge?

Tendrils of hair hung down from an elaborate chignon to touch her neck. He fisted his fingers and shoved them into his pants pockets, resisting the urge to thrust his hands into the silky curls and lift those full lips to his, so he could devour them all over again.

First, he must change the terms of their agreement. He had arranged for them to be wed as soon as they returned to Milan—in a simple civil ceremony, witnessed by a small but exclusive gathering of his friends and associates to avoid any unnecessary press scrutiny. But to convince the Westwick Trustees the marriage was real, he had decided to celebrate the union in an extended, month-long honeymoon on Capri at the palazzo. The symbolism had seemed perfect, but he had come to realise—ever since their kiss—that there was no way he would be able to endure weeks of living there with Tallulah without consummating their fake marriage.

She needed to be aware of his intentions before they took this step. Because he also knew one time would not be enough, not now he had become so obsessed with her.

She watched him—the vivid awareness which had crucified him for days, though, ever since the first time he had touched her in the moonlight, was tempered by that brutal sheen of emotion. And concern.

'How do you wish to change the terms of our agreement?' she whispered again.

He stepped close, to cradle her cheek, then slide his hand around the back of her neck, the desperation to touch her impossible to deny any longer. 'I think you know how, Tallulah,' his said. 'As it is not something I can hide.'

He stroked the rabbiting pulse in her neck, tugged her face up and brought his mouth so close to hers he felt her sharp gasp when the brutal erection pressed against her belly again through their clothing.

'If you do not wish to feed this incessant hunger, now is the time to say so,' he murmured against her lips, his voice hoarse, his fear of revealing too much obliterated by the brutal surge of desire. And desperation.

She stared at him, her lust-blown pupils dilating the blue to black, as he continued to stroke her neck… Waiting for her to admit what they both already knew, desperately holding the need in check to bargain with her if he had to. Already aware he would offer her anything she desired right now to have her.

But instead of demanding more or even asking for clarification of where this would leave their artificial relationship once their marriage became legal, she reached out and fisted trembling fingers in his shirt to draw him closer.

'I… I do want to feed it. I want you, so much.'

The whispered declaration snapped the last thin thread

on his control and the fierce hunger roared through his system.

He dragged her into his embrace, to capture the thundering pulse in her neck with his lips, sucking the soft skin. Finding the curve of her bottom, he caressed the warm flesh, rocking her against his throbbing cock, to ease the pain.

The need swelled. And hardened.

He boosted her into his arms. 'Wrap your legs around my waist,' he demanded, his voice harsh—his need harsher.

She didn't hesitate, cupping his cheeks, raining kisses over his face as he carried her into the bedroom, the ache in his leg for once obliterated by the throbbing agony in his cock. He ground the turgid length against the juncture of her thighs… Desperate to bury himself so deep inside her, he could make the pain go away.

For tonight, at least.

Tali sobbed, her lungs seizing, as Dario tossed her onto the huge bed. The fire in her blood became an inferno as he towered over her. His dark eyes remained fixed on her face, making her skin feel tight, and the swelling heat in her sex ache. He threw off his jacket, then ripped open his shirt, making buttons pop.

'Take off the dress, Tallulah,' he demanded as he tore the shirt free of his trousers and tugged it off. His voice was surprisingly calm and controlled, but the feral harsh command had her racing to obey him.

She tugged the zip under her arm, shimmied out of the expensive satin. But her lungs seized again, her gaze devouring the sight before her when he slung the torn shirt away. His naked chest was as magnificent as the rest of him, the muscles bulging and flexing as he bent his head to unhook his trousers. His pecs were contoured with dark hair that trailed down in a thin line past ridged abs, accentuated by the delicious V of his hip flexors.

He grimaced as he transferred his weight to his bad leg to drag off his trousers. Sympathy echoed in her heart as the crisscross of scars on his thigh was revealed. And she recalled the boy she'd known, lying for weeks in the bedroom in Westwick, insisting the drapes remain closed, often refusing to even acknowledge her presence.

She shook off the sentimental thought when he straightened, her gaze fixing on the thick outline of his erection distending the black briefs.

'The dress, Tallulah,' he said, his voice husky with need. She scrambled to finish taking it off, aware of his hot gaze skating over her bared breasts in the half-light. She folded an arm over her chest, suddenly brutally aware of her nakedness. But when she stood, intending to fold the dress, he grasped her wrist.

'Leave it,' he murmured.

The rich satin dropped from her numb fingers as he lifted her chin with his other hand.

'You are beautiful, Tallulah, you must not hide yourself from me.' The words were gruff, and as commanding as always, but somehow also unbearably romantic, the hunger in his eyes making the hot spot between her thighs burn as he eased her arm down, to expose her fully to his gaze.

His thumb skimmed under a rouged nipple, sharpening the ache between her thighs.

'*Bellissima*,' he whispered, scooping the heavy flesh into his palm and bending to capture the tender peak with his lips.

She sobbed, grasping handfuls of his hair, her breath sawing out in ragged pants as he worked the engorged nipple—with his teeth, his tongue—sucking, stroking, nipping, tormenting… The heat rose and twisted, becoming desperate. He pressed the heel of his hand to her vulva, rubbed her through the sodden lace, then found her swollen flesh, to torture her there, too. One finger, then two, stretched her, stroked her, locating a devastating spot which made her buck against his hold, trying to ride that delicious torment, her body no longer her own.

He murmured something in Italian, his tone gruff.

She clung to him, the pants turning to broken sobs, as the storm built, burned, forcing her closer to the abyss. Her body quaked, but he kept her on that brutal edge, sucking her tender nipples in turn, holding her suspended, tormented, as his fingers drove deep, stretching her, possessing her, retreating to tease and circle her swollen clit but not taking her over.

'Please, I need…' she begged. Too close and yet too far.

'Shh, *bella*, I have you,' he soothed, his voice fierce with the same need tearing her apart.

Then he brushed his thumb over the swollen bundle of nerves. She cried out, breaking into a billion glittering shards of exquisite pain, furious pleasure.

She was still shivering, still shaking, the cloud of afterglow almost as brutal as the titanic orgasm, as he pushed her onto the bed.

She watched him—dazed, dizzy, disorientated—as he dragged off the briefs and freed the massive erection.

She lifted up on her elbows, the desire to stroke him, there, where he was so beautiful, as instinctive as it was unfamiliar. She'd had sex before, but it had never been like this—so stark, so wild, so elemental.

But when she reached for him, he snagged her wrist. 'Do not touch me, Tallulah, I need to be inside you now.'

She swallowed, and nodded, the ache in her throat almost as vicious as the one between her thighs. Why did this feel like so much more than just sex?

'Do I need a condom?' he asked. 'I am clean, I have never taken a woman without one—before you.'

It took her a moment to realise what he was asking—the urgency in his voice an even more powerful aphrodisiac than her recent climax.

'I—I'm clean, too, my only boyfriend was in college, two years ago. And we used a condom, too.'

His eyes flared, the possessive gleam unmistakeable as he hooked his thumbs into her soaked panties and dragged them off. 'And contraceptive?'

'I—I have a coil…' she said, barely able to breathe now, the anticipation building as fast as the emotional storm inside her. And never more grateful in her entire life for the heavy periods which had made the contraceptive device necessary.

'*Grazie a Dio*,' he murmured.

Grasping her hips, he spread her legs to position himself between her thighs. The huge head of his erection butted her sex. She braced, her fingers digging into his broad shoulders as his heavy length slid deep in one devastating thrust.

She groaned, the penetration so huge it was overwhelming. He was wedged to the hilt, stretching her unbearably. But when he pulled out, then rocked back, he went deeper still.

He cradled her cheek, hooked the hair behind her ear from the collapsed chignon. 'It will be okay in a minute,' he coaxed, his tone husky with tension. 'You are very tight.'

She shifted beneath him, trying to ease the pressure,

but brutally aware of the licks of pleasure starting to build again, despite the shocking intrusion.

'And y-you're very big,' she moaned.

The erection twitched inside her as he let out a chuckle.

She writhed again, and his hands tightened on her hips, holding her still, her sex throbbing now in time with her heartbeat, the discomfort receding to be replaced by the driving need to take him even deeper, if that were possible.

'Do not move, Tallulah,' he groaned. 'I do not wish to hurt you.'

She clasped his cheeks, the evening stubble abrading her palms as she stared into eyes as dazed with lust as her own.

'I can't be still. I can't stand it…' she gasped. 'I want you to move.'

He grunted, then pressed his lips to hers, the fierce hunger on his face as glorious as the heavy weight inside her. '*Va bene*, *bella*,' he murmured, the sound rough with relief.

He eased out then back, hitting the spot deep inside her he'd already found with his fingers. But this time, the thick stroke felt hasher, deeper, more devastating, her body's reaction even more powerful, and overwhelming.

'That feels so good,' she moaned.

'*Sì molto buono*,' he groaned back.

Hard hands clasped her hips, the devastating thrusts becoming sharper, stronger, more furious, shooting her towards that desperate peak now with a speed that left her breathless. She clung to his sweat-slicked shoulders, her fingers digging into the muscle to find purchase so she could lift into his thrusts.

She moaned as the brutal orgasm slammed into her at last, her exhausted body shattering, battered by the storm of sensations bursting free. And flew over the edge, as he shouted out his own release, his hot seed pumping into her as he followed her into the abyss.

CHAPTER TEN

DARIO STRUGGLED NOT to collapse on top of Tallulah, his movements clumsy. She let out a staggered moan—her sex still massaging his length through the final throes of her orgasm as he eased out of her body.

He had known their chemistry was extraordinary, but he had never experienced a release so intense, so shattering. He had taken her like a man possessed.

He rolled onto his back, exhausted, even as desire still shimmered through his blood and kept his cock firm.

He had never taken a woman before without protection. Was that it? He tried to rationalise the stunning wave of afterglow. The sense he had just reached a higher plane. Determined it could mean nothing more than sex. But when she shifted next to him, he snagged her arm, not ready for her to leave his side.

'Where are you going?' he asked, his voice groggy as he searched her face for signs of distress.

She had been so tight, but also so wet, so swollen and ready, it had only increased the sense he had never made love to a woman before to whom he was better matched.

Not made love, fucked.

He blinked slowly when she tugged free, desperate to

dislodge the haze of pheromones making it hard for him to breathe, let alone think rationally.

'I… I thought I'd take a shower.' She clasped her arm across her breasts—the pale skin reddened from his attention—as the vivid blush fired across her collarbone.

Damn, had he ever seen anything more arousing?

The polite reply though was contradicted by her panicked expression.

Had she felt it too, the extraordinary strength of their sexual connection? She must have done, although with only one lover before him, she probably had no idea how rare such a connection was. Strangely, the thought of her inexperience helped his frantic heartbeat to slow while his racing thoughts clung to the conviction their connection—however extraordinary—could never be more than sex.

But when she attempted to climb off the bed, he reached for her again.

'Wait, Tallulah… Did I hurt you?' he asked.

The blush brightened, but she shook her head. 'No… I… It felt good.'

He lifted onto his elbow and ran his hand up her arm, to hold her more securely, enjoying her shiver of response.

'Only *good*?' he teased, touched by the way she was blushing so profusely. His heartbeat slowed, the euphoria settling around him when she huffed.

'Okay, very good… I've never had an…' She bit into her lip, clearly not intending to continue.

'You've never had a what, Tallulah?' he asked, smiling, because he could already see the answer in her eyes and feel it in the way her pulse was hammering his thumb. It seemed her only other lover had not been very accomplished.

She tugged her arm free a second time. 'I'm not sure

you need a testimonial, Mr Lorenti… I—I mean, Dario,' she stuttered.

He chuckled, he couldn't help it, the combination of indignation and embarrassment only making her more endearing. *Dio*, had he ever met a woman more delightful, or transparent. Her unguarded reactions were almost as enchanting as the way she responded to him with such raw passion.

He'd been concerned about taking this step. Afraid to want her too much. But *why* had he, when their affair had the potential to make the next few weeks and months so much more satisfying—as well as making it impossible for those infuriating Trustees to deny this was a real relationship? It certainly felt real enough now, in the only way that mattered.

He would never be able to trust anyone enough to commit to more than sex. He never wished to be that boy again, so desperate for friendship he had allowed himself to become too needy, too vulnerable. But indulging this hunger with her…that would be a pleasure.

He'd never been so turned on before. There was something about Tallulah that called to his inner caveman, made him want to protect and possess her at one and the same time, unprecedented reactions which he had never had with the other women he'd dated. But then, he had never met anyone as artless as Tallulah, he decided as he watched her scramble off the bed. She grabbed her discarded dress, using it to cover her nakedness as she dashed into the bathroom.

As her naked bottom disappeared behind the bathroom door, he let out a gruff chuckle. Apparently, her lack of guile only made her more appealing.

He flopped back on the bed. Rubbed his hand over his

chest, no longer disturbed by the rush of heat returning to his cock as he heard the shower.

He had found his fake fiancée's ability to sense his mood disturbing earlier, but why? This attraction was still only a physical connection. And they had all the time in the world to explore it now.

Climbing from the bed, he massaged the ruined muscles of his thigh as he followed her into the bathroom.

She was standing with her back to him in the shower cubicle.

He noticed the tremor in her slender body as she stood under the steamy spray with her hands braced on the glass tiles—making no move to wash herself…

He could almost hear her brain working overtime, probably trying to rationalise what they had just shared.

Good luck with that. There was no way to rationalise something this elemental. The only thing that made sense was to enjoy it, until it faded.

He cleared his throat. Her head shot round, her eyes widening. 'Dario? What are you doing in here?'

But then her gaze shot down to the reaction he could not hide. And her cheeks blazed anew.

Crossing the room, he opened the glass door and stepped into the spacious stone cubicle.

'I thought I would help you wash…' he said, enjoying the shocked awareness which flashed across her features.

Reaching behind her, he lifted the complementary shampoo off the rainfall shower's shelf and poured the fragrant liquid into his palm.

'It's nice of you to offer…' she said, her voice shaky. 'But I'm not sure it's a good idea. It's… It's been a while since I… And well…' Her gaze—wary and tense—slipped down to assess his engorged cock. 'I'm not sure I can do it again so soon,' she finished. He didn't know whether to laugh or wince, the earnest expression on her face only making her more adorable.

He nodded, the regret—that she was probably a bit sore—tempered by the knowledge she had not rejected him outright.

'I am not an animal, Tallulah,' he said, as he pressed her shoulder to turn her to face the tiles again. 'Ignore the erection. I do not expect to have you again tonight. Let me take care of you now.'

'You really don't have…' She began, but then he stroked the shampoo over her wet hair, and she shuddered. A groan broke from her lips when he massaged the flowery liquid into her scalp.

He smiled, his cock throbbing now. *Damn*, but she was so responsive to his touch, it was going to be a struggle to keep himself under control for the rest of the night and make good on his promise not to seduce her again. But as he washed her hair, the soft, silky strands felt exquisite against his palms.

Tonight, he wanted her in his bed, so she could get used to his touch—and he could cure her of the embarrassment.

He had been rough, rougher than he would have liked, all those brutal needs combining after the difficult emotional terrain he had been forced to navigate today.

Yes, she had orgasmed, but he needed to call on every ounce of his finesse, and his expertise with women to ensure he did not scare her off. Wanting her this much would not be a problem, he reasoned, as long as he did not overwhelm her.

He massaged the tight muscles in her shoulders, her staggered moans making his cock pound, and a wry smile form.

Their chemistry was unprecedented, but all that really

meant was their convenient marriage would be much less of a chore than he had anticipated. His smile widened as the water cascaded down and he imagined all the ways he would like to take her in the weeks ahead—once she had recovered from their first attempt.

He dismissed the flicker of regret, that they could never share more than a sexual connection…and ignored the pulsing emptiness inside him… It was better this way.

Tali braced her hands against the shower wall in a vain attempt to control the riot of sensations while Dario kneaded her aching muscles and the heat sank into her sex.

How could he make her want him again so soon, when she was still reeling from the first time. She'd had no idea sex could be so overwhelming, so shockingly intimate. When he'd thrust so deep inside her she'd been able to feel him everywhere, the connection between them had been so fierce, so strong, so devastating it was as if she was making love for the very first time… How could the furtive, fumbling encounter in her college dorm room with… God, she couldn't even recall his name now, her mind in free fall, as another moan escaped when Dario dug into the muscles in her neck.

She dropped her head forward, her breath trapped in her lungs, her legs becoming weightless, her abdomen heavy. The swell of heat making every erogenous zone beg for his touch.

She could feel his erection brushing her back as he worked her shoulders then swept round to cup her breasts. She flinched, when his thumbs brushed her nipples—still tender from his attentions. He stroked the swollen flesh gently.

'Your breasts are very sensitive, Tallulah,' he murmured

against her hair. His voice rumbled across her nape, the tone thick with a strange combination of approval and tenderness. 'I will be more careful next time.'

Next time?

His confidence that there would be a next time only made the twin tides of panic and yearning surge.

She nodded, even as she blinked back the sting of tears. Why was she getting so overemotional? She'd known this would happen, had welcomed it even—because she'd been aroused for days. And the sex had been—she let out a heavy sigh—nothing short of mind-blowing.

Perhaps it was just that she'd never had such an all-consuming reaction to any man before him, never realised sex could be this intense, this powerful. She guessed it was good—to finally discover what all the fuss was about—but she'd also never felt so exposed. Totally and utterly overwhelmed by a physical act, as if her body wasn't hers anymore but his.

She was still dazed, still trying to make sense of it all, when he switched off the water and took her elbow to lead her out of the shower.

She stood, her arms shielding her body, but the shivering was nothing to do with the room temperature, and everything to do with the delayed shock of their joining.

After hooking a towel around his waist, he picked up a large bath sheet and wrapped it around her. She felt like a child, as he dried her overstimulated body in efficient strokes, then lifted another towel off the pile on the vanity to dry her hair.

Why couldn't she say anything? Her arms, her legs, *god*, her whole body felt too sensitive, too alive, and yet also totally exhausted.

Finally, he tucked a knuckle under her chin and lifted her wary gaze to his.

'Are you okay, Tallulah?' he asked, his dark eyes seeing much more than she wanted them to.

'Yes… Yes… I…' She stuttered to a halt, another vicious shiver racking her body. *Oh, for goodness' sake, Tali, stop being such a wuss.* 'I guess I'm just tired. It's been quite a day.'

'Yes, it has.' He smiled, the fierce appreciation in the deep chocolate brown of his irises so validating it scared her even more.

She blinked, hating the renewed tidal wave of emotion which felt like too much. This was just a spectacular booty call. What on earth was wrong with her? Why was she on the verge of tears?

Yes, it had been super overwhelming, in a purely physical sense, and it had the potential to complicate the bargain they'd made…but only if she let her misguided emotions get in the way.

He brushed his thumb across her bottom lip, then clasped her neck, to place his lips on hers. Her tongue tangled with his, the kiss quickly becoming as overwhelming as everything else. But when she braced her hands against his lean waist, needing to steady herself, he drew back.

'Come, you should sleep,' he said, taking her hand in his and leading her out of the bathroom. 'We have a long day tomorrow and there is much we must discuss about our plans for the next few months.'

Months? Really?

She'd been informed by Aldo weeks ago that their wedding—such as it was—had been scheduled for the end of the week once they were back in Milan. That was seven days away. But she'd simply assumed once that was done, she would be able to return to Westwick for a while. The first million euro they'd agreed on would be deposited in the Hall's operating account on their wedding day and she needed to be in Wiltshire to coordinate her plans for the restoration.

But her fuzzy brain couldn't seem to process those considerations enough to be able to broach the subject, especially when they entered the bedroom.

The rumpled sheets—and the sultry scent of sex hanging in the air—had the fierce colour shooting back into her cheeks. The thought of sharing the bed with him all night was somehow even more disturbing to her peace of mind than the memory of the wild, passionate encounter they'd already shared.

She watched, transfixed, as he discarded his towel. He seemed unconcerned by the strident erection, but she couldn't seem to take her eyes off it. The pulse of heat between her thighs becoming catastrophic again, even though she hadn't lied when she'd told him she didn't think she could manage another round tonight.

He nudged her chin up. 'You must stop staring at me like that, Tallulah,' he said the wry amusement making the blush race over her whole body. 'Or I will find it even more agonising to keep my hands off you tonight.'

'I—I could sleep on the couch next door, if you like,' she offered, overwhelmed again.

'It is a good thing my ego is so robust.' He chuckled, his eyes twinkling with amusement, which she suspected might be at her expense.

Had she insulted him by implying he couldn't control himself? Before she had a chance to process the thought though, or voice an apology, crippled by indecision and awkwardness, he whipped off her towel and drew back the sheet.

'Climb in,' he said.

She obeyed without question, grateful for the protection of the bed linens on her naked skin. Instead of joining her, he sat on the bed to tug on his boxers over the still-heavy erection. When he crossed the room and pulled a pair of sweatpants out of his luggage, she felt strangely bereft.

'You're…you're not coming to bed, too?' she asked as he put on the pants, and she tried not to fixate on the scarring on his injured leg…or the deep well of sympathy making her throat tighten again.

He sent her an enigmatic smile—as he grabbed a T-shirt and pulled it over his head.

'Not yet,' he said as he returned to sit next to her on the bed. 'I must walk off the stiffness in my leg…'

'Does the injury still hurt?' she mumbled, swallowing down the dryness in her throat as she recalled the agonising pain he had been in that summer in Wiltshire.

'Only occasionally,' he murmured. But she had the feeling she had crossed a line she was not meant to cross, when the wry smile on his lips did not reach his eyes. 'I am more concerned about the stiffness in other parts of my body, which I must walk off too if I am to keep my promise to you…'

'Oh…okay,' she mumbled, aware of the renewed pulsing in her sex at the bold comment.

'Hold that thought,' he murmured, apparently able to read her mind.

He cradled her cheek, the possessive gesture as overpowering as everything else about him.

Her heart pummelled her chest wall. And it occurred to her that sleeping with him—a man who knew his way around a woman's body and had probably had a ton of these types of booty calls before—had put her at a major disadvantage… Because their fake relationship didn't feel as fake as it should anymore.

He planted a kiss on her forehead. 'Go to sleep, Tallulah. I will see you in the morning. Once we are back in Milan we will discuss the new terms of our arrangement.'

She nodded again. But her heart got wedged in her throat as he walked out of the room, the hitch in his stride more obvious than usual.

She lay in the big bed, willing her pulse to slow down and trying not to think about what he meant by 'the new terms of our arrangement'. The scent of their lovemaking permeated the room, stimulating her already hyperaware senses and doing nothing to dissolve the block of concrete which had got lodged in her throat.

But the whirl of the ceiling fan and the dull hum of the wedding DJ's music—still playing bangers on the other side of the estate—eventually lulled her tired mind and her exhausted body into a deep, drugging sleep.

CHAPTER ELEVEN

Two days later

'...DI AMARTI E ONORARTI *tutti i giorni della mia vita...'* Tali fumbled through the wedding vows in Italian, which she'd had less than forty-eight hours to memorise. She hoped she'd said them correctly. What bothered her more, though, was what they meant.

To love you and every day honour you, for the rest of my life.

Had she really just promised before the officiant and the select gathering of Dario's friends and business associates in his penthouse apartment to love and honour this taciturn and overwhelming man forever?

Of course, that's not what their marriage vows *actually* meant—because she also had the pre-nuptial agreement, putting an end date on their marriage, signed and notarised and stuffed into a pocket of her rucksack. Even so, her stomach rose up to butt her tonsils and her pulse went nuts as Dario gripped her left hand and slid the slim gold band on her finger.

The middle-aged female officiant sent them a hopeful smile, and polite applause echoed around the penthouse's living room. But her hand was still shaking as Dario captured her waist to pull her to him.

The desire darkening his eyes made her breath catch, before he framed her face in his hands and lowered his mouth to hers while the officiant declared them man and wife.

The firm, possessive kiss sent the familiar shock waves hurtling through her system, as he claimed her as his wife, for the benefit of the guests. Her breath backed up in her lungs, the desire like a geyser, raw and real and utterly addictive, even though this was the first time he'd held her since leaving her in the summer house bed two nights ago, alone.

When she'd woken the next morning, he'd already been dressed in a business suit, busy barking orders to one of his assistants in the house's living area. She'd felt like an interloper, the only thing that had stopped her from feeling totally ignored, and weirdly bereft, the knowledge he had slept beside her during the night, because she'd seen the indent of his head on the pillow.

She'd barely had a chance to exchange more than pleasantries with him during the trip back to Milan, because he'd been busy fielding calls in Italian on his mobile or talking to one of his business associates over a video link about a US tech deal, the details of which she hadn't been able to understand. He'd been on his smartphone too, when they'd driven back into the city from the airport, giving her a perfunctory kiss goodbye when the car had dropped her off at her old apartment.

And she hadn't seen him since. Not until fifteen minutes ago, after she'd been informed by Aldo at breakfast this morning, the marriage had been arranged for today, four days ahead of the original schedule. Aldo had at least been apologetic when she'd barely been able to contain her shock. Especially after she'd asked to speak to Dario and his assistant had explained that would not be possible.

What had happened to the discussion about 'our new arrangement' he'd promised her two nights ago? She'd been disturbed at the thought of everything changing between them. But this morning—when a designer had arrived with a cream satin dress, and the beautician and the stylist had been prepping her for a wedding she hadn't even realised was happening today until a few hours ago—she'd wondered what on earth she had been so concerned about… Because it turned out *not* having that conversation was a whole lot more anxiety inducing.

She had no idea anymore what was going on between them. Did he still want her? Why had he arranged the ceremony four days early without informing her? And what was supposed to happen next? Because even Aldo didn't seem to know what his boss's plans were, and all her efforts to contact Dario in the last four hours had gone unanswered.

Aldo had mumbled something about Dario being extremely busy. But when she'd arrived in the penthouse's lobby to find her groom waiting, looking devastatingly handsome in a dark grey tailored suit, and then been immediately whisked into the ceremony, she'd started to feel not just dismayed and wary, but frankly, pissed off.

If he didn't want her anymore, all he had to do was say so…instead of giving her the cold shoulder for forty-eight hours and making her feel like an inconvenient accessory again. What had happened to the man who had washed her hair so tenderly, then tucked her into bed as if she were precious two nights ago?

Her fierce reaction now to his kiss—in front of a crowd of people she didn't know—only humiliated her more.

Why couldn't she control that instant, instinctive response? The way her body melted into his. The way her heartbeat thundered in her ears. The way arousal coursed into her abdomen—and made her sex ache as if he were still lodged inside her. The way her breathing became harsh and ragged—as if she wasn't already disorientated enough after the whirlwind of events in the past two weeks.

When he ended the kiss, she had to lock her knees to stop her legs from shaking. He clasped her hand and lifted her fingers to his lips, the desire so potent in his eyes she felt as if she'd been branded.

He cupped the back of her neck, to tug her towards him until he could whisper against her earlobe.

'*Complementi*, Tallulah. I did not expect you to say the vows in Italian…but you spoke them well.' His gaze darkened, the approval even more disturbing to her peace of mind than his radio silence over the past forty-eight hours. 'Tonight, we can enjoy each other again on Capri. But first we must suffer this charade a while longer.'

Capri? Tonight? What?

She jolted back, feeling overwhelmed again and not in a good way. Everything was moving so fast. While she'd agreed to this *charade*, as he called it, their relationship had changed since their night together in Sicily. Or at least it had for her. She'd assumed he would be more forthcoming about information. If he considered her his lover now, didn't she deserve to be treated like one, instead of just the fake bride he'd hired?

'But…? I thought I would be able to return to Westwick after the wedding…' she managed, suddenly desperate for a time-out. She needed a chance to get her life back on track after Sicily. Obviously, them sleeping together wasn't a big deal for him. But it was for her, enough that she'd been agonising in the last few days about whether he still wanted her—and whether she'd got any closer to knowing whether the connection they shared was more than just sex. She needed to get her volatile emotions under control. If they were going to make this a convenient marriage with benefits, she didn't want to end up getting any more invested than she was already. But the last forty-eight hours had made her feel as if she had stepped aboard a merry-go-round which was accelerating so fast, she might *never* be able to jump off… And she wanted to get off, at least for a few days, to maintain her sanity, before she gave in to this chemistry again.

Dario was just too intense, too…*much*…for someone with her lack of sexual experience to handle, when she felt so powerless.

He frowned. 'You do not wish to return to my bed?' he asked, so candidly her cheeks ignited.

Her gaze darted around the reception. The guests were keeping a respectable distance, to let the happy couple celebrate their new vows in private. But even so, she was taken aback by the direct question.

'That's not what I meant…' she said, because there was no way she could pretend she didn't want him, when her clitoris was pounding in time with her throbbing heartbeat, and she was beathing so hard she was practically hyperventilating from a simple stunt kiss.

'It's just…no one told me we were going to Capri tonight,' she said, trying not to give away how unsettled she felt. Because she was already at enough of a disadvantage.

His smile widened as he caressed the burning skin on her cheek. 'A honeymoon is expected in such circumstances. Is it not?'

A honeymoon? Seriously?

Couldn't he see how problematic that was now they were intimate? A honeymoon would make this union feel far too much like a real marriage…

'Yes…b-but…' she stammered, with no idea what to say. He looked so sure of himself, so unfazed by all of this. She thought she'd sensed some understanding from him that night. Believed he had understood how out of her depth she was after…after they'd… She swallowed, because recalling that night was not a good way to calm her rampaging heart rate. *At all.*

'You should have told me that was the plan…' she said, because suddenly talking about logistics was the only way to control the panic attack she was about to have, at the thought of their not-so-fake honeymoon.

How on earth could she spend days making love to him and remain objective about what their so-called marriage was actually supposed to achieve?

He pressed his finger to her lips then took her hand. 'Let us discuss this in private.'

He gave Aldo a brief nod and then, his grip tightening on her trembling fingers, marched past the guests milling about in the living area, enjoying the cordon bleu appetisers and refreshments which had been prepared by a Michelin-starred chef, and through the doors of the terrace. He nodded brusquely at the two businessmen already enjoying the view, who offered them their hearty congratulations.

'Gentlemen, could you leave us alone? I wish to celebrate with my wife in private.'

Both men nodded, one blushing, and left immediately, closing the terrace doors behind them.

The word *wife*, though, was still echoing in Tali's psyche

when she found herself alone with him for the first time since they had been naked together.

Awkward, much!

The afternoon breeze brushed against her oversensitive skin. She folded her arms around her waist, feeling as if she had just leapt off the high terrace, because her stomach was already in free fall.

He clasped her neck, stroked the pulse point with his thumb, his gaze locked on her burning face. 'Now, tell me what the problem is…'

Where do I even start? Her temper ignited to cover the panic.

'The problem is, I didn't even know we were getting married today until eleven this morning. And what happened to…to…' She paused, not sure how to word the questions which had been piling up for forty-eight hours without sounding clingy, or worse, as if she was expecting more from this arrangement because they had become lovers. 'You said we would discuss this arrangement, how it's going to work, after we became…' She paused, having to push the word out. '*Intimate*. But I haven't been able to speak to you at all.'

'What is it you wish to discuss?' he asked, so matter-of-factly she suddenly wanted to punch him.

Was he really this clueless? But before she could gather her wits about her enough to come up with a coherent answer to *that* asinine remark, he answered it himself.

'The only thing which has changed in this arrangement, Tallulah, is that we will share a bed. We have a rare chemistry which will enhance our time together. This was very clear two nights ago. Do you not agree?'

'Well, yes but…' She stumbled to a halt. She was being railroaded, but she couldn't seem to control all the emotions which were starting to strangle her now to form a coherent argument. Because she wasn't just annoyed and frustrated with him. What did she do with that terrifying spurt of hope, of expectation, which seemed to go well beyond the physical? 'It's just, this is a lot, for me…' she managed. 'I'm not used to being…well…'

She stumbled to a halt again, more exposed than ever. Especially when his dark eyes flared with something fierce and possessive—which only made the spurt of expectation worse.

'I know this, Tallulah,' he said, the tone patient, and more than a little condescending. 'Which is why I have been avoiding you for the past two days. I wished to give you time to adjust,' he added, the husky tone making the pulse in her abdomen become catastrophic. 'Do not worry. We will take this slowly. There is no rush. I have arranged for us to be at the palazzo for a month. There is much I need to do on the island, especially once I take full ownership of the estate—which should be soon. The Trustees were impressed with Lombardi's article, too, and are already convinced this is a real marriage. Having you in my bed will help with this, too.'

His tone had lowered, the husky words and the awareness in his gaze brushing over her skin like a caress. Until one word jumped out at her.

'A *month*? But I can't stay in Capri for a month. What about Westwick? What about my job?' she said, because thinking about her career was so much easier than thinking about how reckless her stupid, delusional heart had already got about this whole situation. 'The money you promised to invest will be deposited today, and I have to be there to oversee the…'

'You will have the opportunity to contact your staff at

the Hall during our stay in the palazzo if you wish,' he cut in. 'There is office space there, and a strong internet connection. But we cannot be apart until the Trustees are satisfied the marriage is valid. Once the ownership has been transferred to me, you will be able to return to Westwick more frequently.'

The pragmatic response had the bubble of hope under her breastbone deflating. This whole thing was still primarily about gaining ownership of the palazzo for him. Because of course it was.

Remember that, Tali. For heaven's sake.

'You have to let me know what's going on, Dario. This isn't just about our… Our…' She swallowed convulsively, feeling hopelessly compromised, even though she knew she shouldn't. 'Our sleeping arrangements. Not anymore. It's also about my work, my life, my choices. I know I signed on to be your stunt wife, but I did that because the Hall is important to me. My work and the people who work there are important to me.' She drew in a heavy breath, not sure she should confide in him, but knowing she wanted to, so he would understand *how* important her work was to her. 'When I was a kid, my father left me and my mum and started another family. For years I tried to get him to see me, to want me, but he wasn't interested. And it crushed me. Moving to Westwick, living there, having a job I loved, working with people I respected, eventually helped me to realise his inability to love me, to even *see* me, was never my fault.'

She blinked, wondering if he could see how that gave them a connection. That they had both been neglected by inadequate men.

But there was one big difference. While she suspected Dario had been determined never to feel too much, her response to that rejection had been to try to make her father come back. And in the process, she'd developed a bad habit of wanting to fix broken things. That's why it had given her so much pleasure making a surly, injured boy smile. But when she'd discovered she was powerless to fix the relationship with her father, no matter how hard she tried, it had destroyed her. Westwick had saved her, eventually. But she couldn't let anyone destroy her confidence again, the way her father had. Not even Dario. *Especially* as she was beginning to sense that despite what Mia had told her in Sicily, Dario had no desire to let her, or anyone else, get too close to him.

Yes, he was a complex and fascinating man, but he also guarded his heart even more fiercely now than he had when he was a teenager.

Perhaps now would be a good time to tell him she'd met him all those years ago. But the fact he didn't know about their history, because he hadn't remembered her, made the confession stick in her throat. Blurting all that out now would only make her feel more exposed, and she was exposed enough already.

He hadn't said anything… But she couldn't tell from his blank expression whether he was shocked or bored or simply dumbfounded by her oversharing… Because his reaction was as inscrutable as always.

Maybe just get to the point then, Tal!

'You *have* to stop ordering me about if we're going to be sleeping together…or it will make me feel…' She sucked in another harsh breath, let it out. 'Powerless again, like I did then.'

He continued to stare at her for the longest time, but when he nodded and then cradled her cheek, to skim his thumb across her skin, his blank expression becoming as tender as it had been that night, the panic finally released its death grip on her chest.

'Your father was *un idiota*,' he said at last.

She huffed out a relieved laugh. '*Absolutamente*,' she murmured, her fledging Italian making his lips curve.

'I apologise for not informing you of my plans sooner,' he added, the tone strained as the smile died. Even so, it felt like a major concession that he'd at least acknowledged she deserved to know what the hell was going on. 'But I want you to come to Capri with me.'

It wasn't really a request, more like a statement of purpose, but it felt vindicating nonetheless—that he had also acknowledged she deserved a choice.

'I... I'll come on one condition,' she countered, determined not to be a total pushover.

She couldn't spend a whole month getting jiggy with Dario Lorenti on Capri without consequences, because that amount of quality time with him was bound to make it next to impossible for her to keep their fling in perspective. He was just so hot and fascinating and demanding, and so unlike any other man she had ever met. Giving herself some time-outs during their not-so-fake honeymoon to visit the team at Westwick and keep abreast of the renovations would help ground her, while also reminding her of the main reason why she had agreed to this arrangement in the first place—to save Westwick, and *not* to indulge in a flaming hot affair with its owner. That was merely a fringe benefit, which she could only come out of unscathed, if she didn't get overinvested in it...and him.

His jaw tensed. He did not look pleased about having to negotiate with her, but instead of attempting to ride roughshod over her wishes for once, which she knew was his default, he simply said, 'And what is this condition?'

She smiled, because it felt like another big win for Team Take-No-Shit Tali.

'I need to return to Westwick for a couple of days each week during our month together on Capri. I want to oversee the new investments being made to the infrastructure in person as well as over the internet,' she rushed on when he frowned, determined to make her request all about Westwick's future and *not* about her insecurities, because it totally was…*mostly.* 'I can do some of that remotely, but my staff also need me to be present.'

The muscle in his jaw hardened. 'You may return once,' he said. 'And for no longer than two days. And not in the first week.'

She sighed, forcing herself to ignore the silly leap in her pulse at how keen he seemed to keep her with him for the whole month.

It's all about fooling the Trustees so he can acquire his palazzo, Tali. It's not you he needs. He just wants to make this marriage look convincing.

She needed to stay focussed now, so she didn't start getting delusional again, and remember her 'marriage' to Dario was a diversion, an adventure, an adrenaline-pumping thrill ride which would end soon enough…

'Okay,' she said. 'I guess I can live with that.' But when she held out her hand for them to shake on it, he grasped her fingers and tugged her into his arms. Cupping her bottom, he caressed her through the satin.

'Our guests are watching, Tallulah,' he said, his gaze fierce with the heated promise which made her pulse bounce, her nipples peak and arousal swell and pound between her thighs.

Then he kissed her so thoroughly, her focus shattered. *Completely.*

Because all she could feel was the insistent erection rising against her belly. And all she could think about was what tonight would hold, once they were finally alone together—and she could climb aboard the adrenaline-pumping thrill ride that was Dario Lorenti…again.

CHAPTER TWELVE

'It's stunning, Dario...'

Pride pushed against Dario's chest at Tallulah's awed comment as the helicopter circled the Palazzo di Constanzo. He tried to catalogue the improvements which had been made since his last visit: the terraces built into the hillside behind the house to create vegetable gardens; the double-level infinity pool which now replaced the old pool which had lain empty and derelict for years; the ornate plastering on the colonnades which had been painstakingly repaired; the recent planting which had come into bloom, the profusion of wisteria and orange blossom adding vibrant splashes of colour to the villa's fanciful frontage.

But his concentration was shot, because his attention was fixed on the woman beside him, and the concerning emotions stirred by the vulnerabilities she had revealed to him on the terrazzo of his Milan penthouse four hours ago.

His heart pulsed, her expression when she had told him about her bastard of a father, was still so vivid—so fierce and yet so open.

The man sounded like even more of a bastard than his own father. How could he have discarded her so easily? But imagining Tallulah as a girl had given him the strange sense that if he could have known her then, he would have wanted to protect her from that rejection, which wasn't just concerning—it was nothing short of ludicrous. Because he had lost the ability to be that man a long time ago, and he had no wish to become that man now.

The flight to Naples had been torture, as he pretended to be engrossed in his cell phone, while being far too aware of his new bride's every sigh, every movement, every breath. Just as he had been forty-eight long hours ago on their return to Milan from Sicily.

Keeping his hands off her until their wedding night had been an exercise in diversion and distraction—and painful denial. It was frustrating to realise starving himself of her company for two days had done nothing to control his addiction.

How could he want her now even more than he had on their night in Sicily?

Especially now he knew how vulnerable she was.

The decision to spend a month at the palazzo had been made after waking up with her lush body wrapped around his in the summer house, his cock so needy it was a miracle he had managed to leave her sleeping. But despite that moment of saintly forbearance, he'd moved the civil ceremony forward as soon as they'd arrived back in Milan, because he'd known he could not wait a whole week to feed this addiction again.

Dio, at least this torture would be over soon.

The helicopter set down on the palazzo's clifftop heliport.

He had wanted to stay at the villa for seven long years but had only had the time for a few cursory site visits—forced to book into a luxury hotel in Ana Capri, the nearby town, while the extensive renovations had been under way. Perhaps seeing the house finally ready was the real cause of this pressure in his chest, as he descended the chopper's steps and held his hand out for Tallulah to follow him—and not the anticipation of a wedding night which only felt real because his new bride looked so perfect.

She wore an elegant pant suit which accentuated her curves, her wild hair tied back with a silk scarf. The new stylist had understood his requirements implicitly—that his wife's wardrobe should not be too revealing. But when the jacket's lapel flicked open in the down draft from the helicopter blades, he got an eyeful of her cleavage, her nipples standing proud against the skimpy camisole beneath, and the familiar pulse of lust blindsided him again.

His hand tightened on hers, touching the gold band he'd placed on her finger that afternoon. Their gazes locked, and the lust swelled when she chewed her bottom lip.

He had requested that the staff prepare an evening meal for them on the main terrace, which overlooked the Bay of Naples, ready for their arrival. With the glow of the approaching sunset reflected in her luminous eyes, he knew he ought to let her eat first, if only to prove he could wait another hour before devouring her. But as the helicopter's blades slowed, he found himself heading instead through the arbour of trees which led to the palazzo's private quarters, charging past the stone walls overflowing with the dark pink blooms of bougainvillea. The subtle honeysuckle scent was one he remembered from the lazy, unstructured days of his childhood, but with her hand clutched tightly in his, and adrenaline pumping through his blood like a drug, the last thing he felt was relaxed.

Finally, they reached the rear entrance. The housekeeper and her staff were waiting for them in the hallway, clearly having assembled to greet his new bride.

But when Tallulah paused to greet them all in Italian,

he found himself tensing. Eventually he was forced to interrupt the introductions—and lead his bride away, not wanting to risk scandalising the staff with his condition.

But he could not wait a moment longer to have her.

'Dario, is everything okay?' Tallulah asked as he marched up the villa's wide sweeping marble staircase to his bedroom suite on the second floor.

As he entered the large sitting room, the salty sea air was tinged with the scent of new paint, but all he could smell was the delicious aroma of her, which had been tantalising his senses ever since he had kissed her on the terrazzo in Milan.

He could still taste her arousal. And he intended to focus on that now, and not the emotions which had made him want to protect that neglected girl.

The terrace doors stood open to let in the evening breeze. The dying daylight added a golden glow to the spectacular view of the Tyrrhenian Sea from the palazzo's enviable position as the lights of Ana Capri twinkled in the distance.

He had waited so long to come here again. To return to the only place he had ever been truly happy. The work he had paid for—hiring the best local craftsmen and artisans to return the palazzo to its former glory, long before the heady days of his mother's endless parties, or his father's deliberate neglect—was finally complete. And it was only a matter of time now before he would own the place outright.

Why then did he feel almost ambivalent about what this marriage had always been supposed to achieve? It was almost as if he couldn't appreciate the beauty of the palazzo and the stunning vista through the terrazzo doors, because the only beauty he could see was Tallulah, her arms wrapped around her midriff, her breasts straining against the silk camisole, the mess of her curls highlighted by the dying sun when she took off the scarf.

His breath clogged in his lungs as the heat surged.

'Do you wish to eat?' he made himself ask. But there was no mistaking the husky desire in his voice.

She shook her head, trembling. 'I don't think I could eat anything at the moment,' she said, her blue eyes shining with that exquisite combination of awareness and sincerity—which he had become obsessed with.

'Are you cold?' he asked, trailing his thumb down her neck to stroke the pulse point hammering her throat.

The muscles jumped as she swallowed, her wary gaze only intensifying the hunger making his cock throb.

'Actually, I think I'm the opposite,' she murmured, her meaning clear.

He chuckled, the sound rough with need. *Dio*, but she was so forthright, her honesty almost as compelling as the colour blooming across her collarbone.

'*Bene*,' he murmured.

Spreading her jacket open, he grasped her waist to draw her into his arms. Capturing her lips, he thrust his tongue deep—to claim her shocked sob. Her nipples thrust against his chest through their clothing as he devoured her mouth, exploring the hidden recesses, capturing each heady sigh, each sweet shudder.

He tore his mouth free, so they could each drag in a shattered breath.

'I cannot wait to have you again, Tallulah. But I promise to be gentle.'

She nodded, the trust in her eyes crucifying him all over again.

Did she have any idea how wild he was for her? He hoped not. But he could not control himself much longer, the tormenting desire to brand her as his fast becoming all-consuming.

Perhaps she was not his real wife—perhaps he had never intended this relationship to be more than a means to an end. But when she allowed him to strip off the jacket, to cup her breasts through the silk, and close his mouth over those yearning peaks, his intentions didn't matter. Her fingers sank into his hair, her back arching instinctively to thrust the engorged nipple into his mouth, and he knew he had never needed anyone the way he needed her. Right now.

He scooped her into his arms, heard her harsh gasp as he strode through the living area, his aching leg nowhere near as painful as his swollen cock.

A new four-poster bed dominated the suite's main bedroom, the other furniture artfully arranged around it, the terrace doors opening onto a dappled view of the coastline and the pure blue sea enhanced by the sunset.

But he couldn't see any of it, because all he could see was her, as he laid her trembling body on the satin bedspread, then proceeded to undress her, the promise to be careful a whole new form of torture.

He tugged off her camisole, her bra, the sleek trousers, her lacy panties with frantic, clumsy fingers… Within seconds she lay naked, her pale skin rosy with heat, the musky scent of her arousal intoxicating him. He stripped off his shirt, and watched her eyes darken as her gaze skated over his chest.

But then she clasped an arm over her breasts.

'*Non*… Do not cover yourself…'

Her eyes widened at the harsh demand, but she let her arm drop.

He swallowed, knowing he had to calm down to make this good for her.

Climbing onto the bed, he took her arm, kissed her fingers, then trailed his tongue along the sensitive skin inside her elbow, across her collarbone, to circle her stiff nipple. Lifting her breast, he fastened his lips on the pouting tip and suckled hard.

She groaned, bowing back, her sobs like a whip to his senses.

He worked one breast, then the other, trapping her tender flesh against the roof of his mouth, entranced by her instant, unguarded response. Had any woman ever been so attuned to his needs, so quick to meet his demands with demands of her own?

He brushed his fingers into the curls covering her sex, and coaxed the slick folds open, to locate the plump nub of her clitoris. He circled it, testing her readiness, aware of the painful erection already threatening to burst out of his pants.

'Dario… Oh… God…' She writhed, each teasing touch making her buck, until she was riding his hand, desperate for relief.

Finally, he gave her the sure solid touch she craved. And watched, enthralled, his own body already on the brink, as she shattered.

She was still trembling, as she opened eyes slumberous with afterglow. He staggered to his feet, to wrestle off the rest of his clothing. Naked, *finally*, he rolled her onto her stomach and dragged her onto her knees until he could probe her glistening sex from behind.

He didn't want to see her face, couldn't let himself get lost in those bright, bliss-shattered eyes, in case he again saw the vulnerability she had shown him that afternoon.

She let out a staggered groan as he drove deep, her recent orgasm allowing him to bury himself to the hilt in a single thrust. He held her hips—to pull out, and pound back—forcing her to take the full measure of him. The tight clasp of her sex massaged him in rhythmic beats as he began to move.

Her cries of fulfilment became rawer and more elemental. Finding her clit, he worked it, ruthlessly, forcing her over again, his own climax building like a tsunami.

The burning heat seared through him, scorching him in brutal waves, the driving need building to a blistering crescendo. His movements became jerky, uncoordinated as the devastating orgasm slammed through him—fast, furious, unstoppable—and he emptied himself inside her at last.

Tali fell forward onto the mattress, her body shaking with the vicious power of her orgasm… Make that *orgasms*…

Dario's big body collapsed on top of her.

How many orgasms had she had? Because it felt as if each one had layered on the last, until the brutal mindless waves of pleasure had become never-ending.

He was still firm inside her, the penetration still deep. But then he lifted off her. She moaned, the blissful afterglow only intensifying the strong sense of loss.

She'd been looking for a connection with him, but maybe this incendiary connection was all they would ever share.

The rasps of their breathing slowed, and the afterglow faded, but the painful regret remained, snaking around her chest to squeeze her ribs.

He touched her cheek. 'Look at me, Tallulah,' he murmured, the demand softened by the husky tone.

She made herself meet his gaze in the half-light, trying to disguise her reaction.

This is just your first multiple orgasm talking, Tali. That's all.

Lit by the setting sun, his handsome features looked stark, the red glow accentuating the scar on his cheek.

Why did that make her heart squeeze?

'*Bene*?' he asked.

'*Sì, molto bene*,' she said, replying automatically in Italian.

A smile lifted his lips, making his harsh features look almost boyish. The fierce approval in his eyes made her throat close.

She placed her palm on his scarred cheek, needing to acknowledge their connection, however misguided.

'*Amo quando mi fai amore*,' she murmured, hoping she'd said what she'd meant to say, correctly.

I love when you make love to me.

Eager for him to know that much at least.

But she wasn't sure she had said it right, when his cheek tensed and the smile disappeared.

For a moment he looked so much like the surly teenager she remembered, hiding his pain behind a mask of indifference, she almost pulled her hand away. But the desire to reach him was a compulsion she couldn't control either, even though she knew she should.

'This is good,' he said, but the change into English felt like another attempt to create distance. 'It will make our honeymoon more enjoyable.'

He covered her hand and drew it away from his face, destroying the moment of intimacy. But his avoidance only made her more determined to ask the question which had been lodged in her brain for weeks—ever since he'd told her why he needed this marriage.

'Why is owning this house so important to you, Dario?'

His gaze remained fixed on hers. But she could sense him calculating whether or not to give her an answer… It felt like a blow, to know he still didn't trust her with even the most innocuous details of his past, when she had trusted him with some of the most personal details about hers earlier that day.

But she tried not to overreact. He hadn't asked for those confidences, and while their wedding vows had felt oddly real while they had made love—the fierce euphoria reinforcing the elemental connection they shared—that was surely just an illusion caused by the intense endorphin rush of multi-orgasmic sex.

As she waited though, for him to brush away the question, the foolish hope for more turned her stomach to mush.

He flopped onto his back and flung an arm over his eyes. But just when she was sure he was going to shut her out again, he began to speak. The wry monotone was carefully devoid of emotion. But somehow, she sensed that the only way he could reveal even this much to her was by pretending it didn't matter to him anymore.

'I lived here as a boy, with my mother and sister. Mia was so young when my mother died, I'm not sure she remembers much of it… But I do.' He lowered his arm, turned towards her and let out a huff of breath, which was supposed to sound amused, but all Tali could hear was the echo of despair. All she could see was the shadow of the intense emotions he was so desperate to hide in his eyes… 'She was so full of life, but also so volatile, her emotions swinging from elation to desperation, often in a single day. But our life here was always colourful, never dull thanks to the parties she hosted every night because she hated to be alone. The villa was always full of people. And she loved us, very much.'

'That sounds a bit chaotic for a child.' And terrifying. Children might think they loved freedom, but they also needed structure to feel safe. She wondered how a boy—who now maintained such a rigid control over his emotions as an adult—had coped with so much insecurity.

He shrugged. 'Yes, it was precarious at times, but it was also exhilarating.'

'How so?' she probed, touched by his willingness to share something too… But also desperately curious about the glimpse he was giving her of the boy Mia had described, before his father, and his accident, had sucked all the joy out of his personality.

'There were no boundaries, no rules,' he murmured, his features softening with memory. 'She spent all the money he gave her after the divorce on luxury food, the best wines and champagnes, and party drugs. Of course, she frequently forgot to pay the staff—and the electricity bill. Mia and I often wore shoes which didn't fit because practicalities bored her. But we dined on lobster and calamari fritti for breakfast and could stay up all night if we wished.'

'Didn't she ever take a night off?' Tali asked, knowing most children would have struggled to survive such an upbringing.

Did he really remember his childhood with only fondness, when he had created such a rigid structure to his own life since?

He propped himself on an elbow, his gaze intense as it roamed over her face. 'You do not approve?'

'It's just… It sounds a little scary and chaotic.'

He frowned. 'It was, at times, but my life here made me self-sufficient, so I cannot regret it,' he said, but the sadness that remained in his eyes told a different story. Of a boy who had been forced to fend for himself—and his sister—from a very young age. Who had never been nurtured, by either of his parents.

He huffed out a breath. 'What was much harder was being forced to leave Capri, by my father. He closed the house up after my mother's death and left it to rot. Then stuck Mia and me in boarding schools, where they did not want me to think for myself. My father expected obedience and loyalty, while he did nothing to earn it.'

'You still hate him?' she murmured, although she already knew the answer. It had made her sad for him as a little girl to witness his father's lack of interest in him, or his recovery. She recalled the only time Westwick had come to visit his son, the angry words and harsh criticism she had overheard as she hid behind the wardrobe door still burned in her memory. It had made her more determined to become his friend even though he'd shouted at her after his father had left to leave him the hell alone, clearly holding back tears. But it made her even sadder now, to know his hatred of his father had stopped him from allowing that boy to heal the rest of the way.

'I feel nothing for him,' he said dismissively. 'As you should feel nothing for yours. It is pointless to waste your love on people that will not love you back.'

'I suppose,' she said, aware of the warning note in his voice. But also knowing she didn't agree with him.

She'd eventually had to admit her dad was a lost cause, to protect herself from being hurt any more. But how could love ever be wasted? That she had wanted to repair that relationship wasn't a bad thing, and neither were her attempts to be Dario's friend when he'd so desperately needed one. Even if she now knew she'd failed at that too, because he hadn't even remembered her.

But she was still glad she'd tried.

James Westwick had been an inadequate parent at best, even worse in some ways than her own, because his children hadn't had a mother the way she had… But she wondered if Dario's mother, when she'd been alive, had really been that much better. Maybe she had loved her children in her own way, but it didn't sound as if she had ever put their welfare first.

'How did your mother die?' she asked, recalling the flicker of pain which had crossed his face when he'd mentioned her death.

One sceptical eyebrow arched. The grief ruthlessly quashed.

'Really? You have not done an internet search on me?'

'No,' she murmured, hoping he wouldn't ask her the reason why. Because her desire to find out more about him from *him*, instead of a bunch of news headlines, would probably convince him she was impossibly sentimental, even naïve.

'She overdosed one night, by accident. The staff found her in the morning,' he said so dispassionately, she shivered.

'I'm… I'm so sorry, Dario,' she said, tears stinging her eyes.

He brushed away the single drop which escaped with his thumb. The puzzled expression on his face was worse, though, than the thought of him as a boy, losing his mother so needlessly.

'Do not cry, it was a long time ago.' His gaze became shuttered, before his thumb traced the line of her collarbone. 'This is hardly conversation for our wedding night,' he murmured.

Except it's not really our wedding night, because this isn't supposed to be a real marriage.

It's what she should have said, but then he dipped his thumb under the sheet, to circle her nipple, and she lost her train of thought. Heat arrowed down to her core as the swollen peak hardened.

He leaned closer to place his mouth on the pulse point in her neck. He suckled the sensitive skin, while his hand sank further beneath the sheet to flatten over her belly then drag her to him, until his erection brushed her thigh.

'Can you take me again?' he asked, the gruff demand making her sex clench and release, already desperate to be filled.

'Yes.' She clasped his cheeks, to drag his head up and kiss him. She explored his mouth, as he shifted her weight, until he was wedged between her thighs again, probing at her entrance.

He impaled her in one punishing thrust, taking her breath away, even as her misguided heart battered her rib cage.

Why did this feel like so much more than it should?

But as he established a rhythm, angling her pelvis to drive deeper still, the coil of need clenched tight, thrusting her back towards that vicious edge with startling speed… She gave herself up to the shattering pleasure, desperate to ignore the demands of her eager heart—and the yearning to have him need her, for more than sex.

But as she lay in his arms afterwards, his fingers skimming her breast, his heart thumping against her ear, the bubble of hope expanded again.

Because it wasn't just the sex which felt earth-shattering

anymore, it was the knowledge that however wary Dario was of intimacy, however desperate not to let himself care too much for anyone again—after *both* of his parents had hurt him—this demanding, taciturn man had trusted her enough tonight to show her why he guarded his heart so fiercely.

And if he could trust her with that much…was it foolish to think that one day, he might be able to trust her with more?

CHAPTER THIRTEEN

Two weeks later

'THE ROOF REPAIRS will be finished by next week, the slate loss wasn't as bad as they thought. And the interior decorators are starting on Monday. They wanted to run a few things by you about the cornices in the East Wing ballroom.'

'That's fabulous, thanks, Ellie. Send me the details and I'll take a look.' Tali beamed at her acting estate manager through the video link. 'You're doing an amazing job, and I really appreciate the daily updates.'

'And I really enjoy you making sure I'm not mucking anything up.' Ellie grinned. 'How's the honeymoon going? It's all so romantic. I still can't believe you married him so quickly. It's so exciting. And he's so handsome.'

Tali felt her face heat—at the memory of their lovemaking that morning. After two weeks, her sexual connection with Dario had only got hotter. But more than that, Dario had turned out to be a surprisingly attentive and involved fake husband, out of bed, too.

Each day—after they'd both checked in with their work—he had some new excursion to suggest. They'd been snorkelling in the villa's lagoon and taken out his sailboat most days—as he tried, and comprehensively failed, to teach her how to sail. He'd insisted on escorting her on a couple of day trips to Ana Capri, a delightful and surprisingly quiet town less than a mile away, where they had whiled away hours exploring the shops or lunching at the local trattorias, binging on homemade pasta—before they drove home on his motorbike to binge on each other again. He enjoyed her company, as well as the sex. And she adored discovering all the reasons why he loved this place so much. And if her attempts to explain why she felt the same way about Westwick hadn't exactly persuaded him, it was all good, because whenever the subject of the Wiltshire estate came up, he usually insisted on diverting the conversation with mind-blowing sex.

She'd come close a couple of those times to blurting out how long she'd lived at Westwick, because she wanted him to know she understood his reluctance to return to the estate, that she knew how hard those months had been for him after the accident. But she'd stopped herself, deciding it felt like poking at a wound she had no right to poke at.

He hadn't shared more about himself, about his thoughts and feelings, since their conversation on their first night here. In fact, he'd kind of avoided talking about anything deep with the same diligence and determination with which he made love to her… But she refused to worry about it. They were getting on so well, it felt like more than enough—for now.

'Will you guys be living at Westwick once the honeymoon's over?' Ellie's enthusiastic question cut through Tali's latest revelry…

She cleared her throat. It wasn't the first time Ellie had asked the question—no doubt her assistant thought it was beyond odd Tali was still keeping her position as Westwick's estate manager when she was now supposedly married to the owner. But this time the standard reply she'd been giving Ellie, and everyone else—that nothing had been confirmed yet—got stuck in her throat. She hated lying to her staff about the relationship, perhaps because their marriage had begun to feel like more than a fake arrangement to her, too.

Every time Dario touched her with that hot glint in his eyes that told her he needed her. Each time he clasped her hand in his while they were sightseeing, or shopping, or simply lying on the estate's private beach enjoying the sunset. Whenever he praised her faltering Italian or kissed her with enough passion and purpose to make her yearn for the hard drive of his body into hers. Every time he insisted on showing her some new place, or looked at her as if she fascinated him, or pressed his lips to her knuckles while teasing her, the tender gesture in sharp contrast to the fierce intensity with which they always ended up making love… She became that little bit more invested, that little bit more convinced that something real was happening between them.

But how did she make him acknowledge that this was more than either of them had intended, if their relationship still had an end date…and she didn't even have the guts to have a conversation with him about returning to Westwick for a few days, like they'd agreed?

She was beginning to realise she needed to soon, more than ever. Because as much as she'd loved the past two weeks, which had flown by in a haze of pheromones and intimacy, how could this be more when the marriage—and her life here—was still effectively a stunt to fool the Trustees? She had to bring herself back down to earth to figure out if her growing attachment to Dario was more than just the adrenaline rush of great sex and having his undivided attention. Because there was no doubt about it, the man was intoxicating, especially now she was getting more tantalising glimpses of the boy he had been before his mother's death—wild and free, his spirit undimmed by his father's neglect and judgement.

But he was still so unwilling to even think about Westwick, her updates on the Hall's progress always instantly dismissed. And he still hadn't contacted Mia and Sante, to heal the rift with his best friend the rest of the way…

She sighed. 'Honestly, Ellie. I'm not sure where we'll be living in the long term. But I'm heading back to Westwick on Monday.' She pushed the words out, knowing that if she made it official, it would force her to talk to Dario. It was past time for her to call in that promise.

'Oh wow, really? That would be amazing. Will Mr Lorenti be coming with you?'

'Ummm…' The left-field question had the bubble of hope pushing against her breastbone again. It would be amazing if Dario came with her. Not only would it show a commitment to the Hall, but it would also be a commitment to her. To *them*… Whatever *they* were.

But then she got a clue. Dario hated Westwick… The priority now was to stop letting Dario have everything his own way. And to give herself space to figure out what was really going on between them.

Because she was afraid she was already more than halfway in love with her fake husband… And she still didn't really have a solid idea how he felt about her.

Going back to her real life, regrouping, rebooting, giving herself a purpose again—beyond the pursuit of endless pleasure—if only for a few days, would give her that much-needed perspective.

And standing up to Dario might finally give her the courage and the confidence to tell him about the past they shared…and how much their fake marriage was starting to mean to her.

'The Trustees signed the papers necessary to give you full ownership of the property and the estate two hours ago, as per the terms of your father's will. Congratulations, Mr Lorenti. The palazzo should be yours officially by this time tomorrow when all the necessary documents have been filed with the court.'

Dario nodded, as the head of his legal team in London smiled at him as if he had just won the lotto. But the euphoria he should be feeling eluded him.

'There is no chance they will renege on this position?' he asked.

The solicitor frowned. 'They can try if they want, but the property is yours now, not much they can do about it. I guess they could sue, but it would be a lengthy process, and costly. And I doubt they'd want to risk their own money on any further legal action against you. Why do you ask?'

Because the marriage is not real.

It felt too easy, after seven years of legal wrangling, to have the Trustees release their stranglehold on the palazzo after only a month. The deception had given him what he had wanted. But the very first thought that came into his head was not how easily he had bested those old fools in the end—it was disappointment at the thought he would now be able to release Tallulah from the terms of their agreement sooner than planned.

He would not divorce her until the end of the year. He might own the palazzo, but he did not want to encourage a lawsuit, if the Trustees realised they had been duped into signing over the property.

But there was no tangible reason to remain here, pretending to have a honeymoon. No reason why his 'wife' could not return to her life in England, and he to his home in Milan in the next few weeks.

The only problem was, every single cell in his body rebelled against the idea of letting her go…

It's the sex. It has to be.

He still had not had his fill of her. That was all. Even though they had been making love every morning and night and so many snatched moments in between for two weeks now, he still wanted her, incessantly—to the extent that even when they were not making love, he enjoyed being with her. She fascinated him and enchanted him. He felt like a teenager again, the boy who had been starved of affection, and now he wished to gorge on it to his heart's content. Because Tallulah was just so *kind…*

He swallowed, the thought of how artless and engaging and delightful she was, both in and out of bed, even more disturbing than the thought of letting her go.

She was so open. So tender. So compassionate. So genuine. He'd never before met a woman so positive and honest and undemanding. And because of that, she had become a fire in his blood.

Of course, this fire would burn out eventually. He already suspected sometimes when she looked at him, she wished for more from him. And a part of him understood, as he held her late at night, while she slept beside him, her open and tender heart would become bruised eventually when she fully accepted there could never be more between them.

But this fire had not burnt out yet. Plus, she had agreed

to remain on Capri for at least a month, so why end this arrangement prematurely, when they were both enjoying it? It had been years since he'd taken a genuine break from work… And now the estate was his, why should he not enjoy the fruits of the labours to bring it back to life?

'Good work, Carstairs,' he said.

'By the way, our real estate department has a buyer for Westwick,' the man said. 'It's a Saudi investment conglomerate. They want to turn the place into a resort hotel, which would probably mean some substantial remodelling. We've looked at the building's status on the heritage registry, and apparently it's only the frontage that's listed, the rest of it can be demolished and rebuilt. Anyway, it's a great offer. You want me to set that in motion?'

Again, the news should have been like having all his birthdays come at once. The Hall still held so many unpleasant memories for him, those long days spent festering in the bed after his accident. It represented everything about his childhood he had always hated—his father's searing contempt, the loss of his mother, the loss of his life on Capri, the loss of his freedom… But in the past two weeks, every time Tallulah mentioned the Hall, which she did quite often, he had begun to understand a little more how much the place really meant to her. And there had been other memories that had tickled the back of his consciousness. The little girl who had been so determined to coax him out of his shell, whose presence and bright, lively friendship had eventually made that long, unhappy summer bearable.

It made him feel weak and foolish to remember that girl now, and how much he had come to depend on her daily visits to his sickbed. And in some ways, Tallulah's love of Westwick made him hate the place more too—because he knew she would want to return there once their time together was over. But could he bring himself to take the one thing away from her that he knew she cared for so passionately?

He had turned himself into a cold and ruthless man over the years, deliberately. So he would never be that scared, lonely boy again. But sometimes, late at night, with her beside him, he had allowed his mind to wander, enough to even question how happy the isolation he had imposed on himself since that summer had made him. After all, letting his resentments, his anger fester, had allowed him to believe his father's lies about Sante for too long. So long in fact, he now found it impossible to return the calls and messages from both him and Mia, inviting him to return to Sicily.

Similarly, how could he take the one thing away from Tallulah she had wanted out of this whole arrangement, when they parted? And what if he did not wish to cut ties entirely? Having her working for him would give him an excuse to see her again, should he wish.

'Hold fire on that for now,' he said, suddenly feeling almost sentimental about Westwick.

'Are you sure?' Carstairs looked astonished. 'I don't know how long the deal will be on the table, Mr Lorenti.'

'I'm sure there will be other interested buyers if I decide I still wish to sell,' he heard himself say before ending the call abruptly.

He could never live in the Hall, but Tallulah seemed devoted to the place and the people she worked with there. And surely, he owed her that much, for helping him secure ownership of the palazzo.

Although strangely, since he'd been here with her, he'd also become aware that the idyllic memories he had of

Capri had always been overshadowed by other emotions he'd been careful to lock away since. As a boy he'd adored the freedom, but hadn't he also been in constant fear that his mother's dark moods would come back, that Mia would not have enough to eat? The staff had come and gone with alarming regularity because his mother squandered the money to pay their salaries on her endless pursuit of pleasure at all costs. And the house and its grounds had been in a deteriorating state long before her death, the wild parties often becoming scary when the adults were all either drunk or drugged up to their eyeballs.

His money had repaired the property, but Tallulah's presence had added a layer of something more… Companionship, friendship, stability even, that he hadn't realised he had yearned for then, until these past two weeks.

He blinked, the sentimental thoughts somehow lowering his guard.

Dio, when had he become so soft?

The light knock had him turning to find Tallulah standing on the threshold of his office. Something swift and sharp rushed through him.

Why was he so overjoyed to see her, when they had made love less than two hours ago?

'Dario, I need to speak with you,' she said.

He strode towards her and grasped her around the waist, deciding that fierce rush could only be the desire to have her again. To feed this damn addiction. She wore a simple summer dress, making it easy for him to lift the skirt and palm her lush flesh, even as he dragged her the rest of the way into the room and slammed the door closed with his foot.

'How about we talk later?' he said, sinking his hands into her panties to cup her naked bottom.

She gasped, but if she was shocked by the demand, the scent of her arousal that filled his senses told him her answer. He clasped her hand, strode to the desk, and pushed the laptop and papers to one side to lift her onto the surface…and inhaled the sultry scent which told him she wanted him with the same intensity.

He covered her mouth with his, to swallow her sob of surrender and found the hot flesh between her legs with insistent fingers. She moaned, lifting her arms to rope around his neck, while he worked the swollen erection free of his pants.

'Yes?' he asked, even though her eyes were already dazed with need.

She nodded, and he clasped her hips to thrust his straining cock into her, the penetration impossibly deep.

They rode the sharp, swift wave to completion in a matter of seconds, her orgasm massaging him to his own fierce release, their ragged breathing reverberating around the quiet room. The heady mix of need and desperation disturbed him as he felt his heartbeat start to slow and her hands shaking where she gripped his shoulders.

He buried his face in her hair, suddenly ashamed of the vicious hunger he hadn't even attempted to control.

What was wrong with him? She wasn't just a fire in his blood now—she had become someone he couldn't seem to live without for more than a few hours at a time.

She shifted slightly, still impaled on the rigid length. He pulled free of her body and felt her flinch. The shame twisted in his gut like a blade.

He raised his gaze to hers, cradled her cheek to press a kiss to her temple.

'I apologise, Tallulah, that lacked finesse,' he managed,

which had to be the understatement of the century. He had treated her as if he were a rutting bull.

Her face was flushed, her lips trembling, and yet the smile which crossed her face was unbearably sweet. 'Don't apologise, Dario. I—I love it when you need me like that.'

He stepped back to repair his clothing. How could she be so artless, so innocent and yet affect him so deeply?

She climbed off the desk and lifted her torn panties from the floor, before shoving them into the pocket of her dress.

Dio, had he ripped her underwear from her? How had this need become so wild, so elemental?

'What did you wish to talk about?' he asked, forcing his mind to engage again through the fog of pheromones and panic.

She stared at him blankly, her lust-blown pupils hazy with confusion.

Good to know he wasn't the only one blindsided by this hunger.

She blinked. 'Oh, yes… I wanted to return to Westwick tomorrow—just for a few days.' For a moment the information would not compute in his endorphin-addled brain. 'The decorators are arriving on Monday, and I need to be there to oversee the work.' She hesitated then rambled on, making no sense. 'I've arranged a flight from Naples. I was wondering if I could borrow one of your cars and park it at the airport…'

She continued to babble about her travel arrangements as frustration rose up inside him.

'No…' He barked the word more harshly than intended, making her jumbled information slam to a halt. 'You cannot leave Capri yet.'

Because I still want you, all the damn time.

Thank god he managed to bite off that confession before it could tumble out of his mouth. But the fear continued to claw at his chest. He could not let her go, not yet. He wasn't ready.

Her eyes widened. But then her chin firmed, and he saw the stubbornness which had been absent for the last two weeks… It was annoying to realise he'd missed it.

'We agreed, Dario, in Milan, on the day we exchanged vows,' she said, with a patience that infuriated him. Did she think him an imbecile, that he didn't remember that? 'And you…you promised.'

He let his frustration build, to control the panic. He didn't want her to go. What if she did not come back? He needed her.

Even as the thought struck him, the walls of the study, bright with the mid-morning sun, seemed to close in around him. His leg throbbed, alongside the scar on his face… And he was suddenly that boy again, trapped in the wreckage of an overturned car, waiting forever for his only friend to return to him.

He stalked across the room, turning his back to her, to stare at the rocky coastline, the shimmering blue of the sea, the glint of the cliffs, the rambling pinks and purples of the bougainvillea, his body still humming with afterglow, his stomach hollowing out.

He thrust his fingers through his hair, trying to buy himself time, to control the fear, the emotion, that hideous feeling of being abandoned, of being alone.

'I'll be back in a few days…' she murmured.

He swung round. 'No, I will accompany you,' he managed, his throat still raw with panic, the sweat pooling to run down his spine. 'We will take the helicopter to Naples, and the jet from there to Heathrow. Then we can transfer by car to the estate.'

Even as he suggested the hasty travel plan, he knew he sounded deranged. The last damn thing he wanted, the last damn thing he had *ever* wanted, was to spend time at Westwick. But how could he force her to stay? Not only had he promised to let her return to Wiltshire during the month, but worse, it would make him seem weak and too needy to refuse her request.

Her face softened with surprise and then a brilliant smile crossed her features.

'Really? You'll come to Westwick with me?'

'Yes, of course. We must not separate yet, the Trustees still need to be convinced this marriage is real,' he said, the white lie coming easily.

'Oh Dario, that's wonderful.' She rushed towards him and wrapped her arms around his waist. He clasped her shoulders, stupidly touched by her transparent, and uncomplicated reaction. And ignored the prickle of guilt that she had accepted his lie so readily. Because her blind faith in him, and her trust, however undeserved, was somehow even more intoxicating than the furious lovemaking, the effects of which still echoed in his groin. As she began to reel off a list of things she wanted to show him—to do with the renovations—he didn't have the heart to tell her the truth, that he had no interest in the Hall. But as she continued to babble, the brutal thunder of his own heart, crashing against his ribs, started to ease.

He would take her to that godforsaken place, and then bring her back here with him… And keep her here, until he could lock the fear away again for good.

Then, at last, he would be able to let her go.

CHAPTER FOURTEEN

DARIO STARED OUT of the window of the chauffeur-driven limousine, which had picked them up at Heathrow two hours ago, as it drove through the gates of Westwick Hall. The last time he'd been here, he'd only had to stay for a matter of minutes. But now he would have to remain for several days. The thought did not appeal to him, the hollow sensation he had been running away from for years making his stomach drop to his toes.

But as the large Palladian frontage came into view—the twin staircases which led to the front entrance obscured by scaffolding—he found himself glancing at the woman asleep beside him.

She had been talking non-stop when they had boarded the jet that morning in Naples, keen to apprise him of all the different infrastructure projects she had put in motion with the investment he'd given her… How had that simple bribe—to get her to marry him—become so damn complicated in the weeks since? He'd started kissing her—mostly so he could shut her up about Westwick. But of course, as soon as he'd touched her, tempted her, she'd responded with the artless enthusiasm he found so intoxicating… And before either of them could say 'mile-high club' they'd been tearing each other's clothes off in the jet's bedroom.

He could see now he'd exhausted her, because she'd fallen asleep as soon as they'd driven away from the airport.

Her enthusiasm about this place had only deepened the chasm in his stomach which had been growing ever since he had agreed to this trip. With her scent filling the car, though, and the thought of what lay ahead when they arrived at the Hall, it was impossible for him to switch off his brain…or the memories which continued to torment him.

The chauffeur braked on the newly laid driveway in front of the towering edifice of his father's house. Even with the May sunlight glinting off the recently sand-blasted stonework, the place loomed over him—oppressive and judgemental—a miserable reminder of the grieving child, and the broken teenager he'd tried so hard to destroy. Why did this place always yank him back to those times in his life when he'd felt so powerless and alone?

Except he wasn't alone now, he thought, as he glanced at Tallulah, her head nestled on his chest. He pressed a kiss to her hair, knowing he should control the pleasure which welled inside him like a drug—but not quite able to today, while the shadow of his past lay over him like a shroud.

'Wake up, bella,' he murmured to Tallulah as a young woman bounded out of the house, a smile of welcome on her face, followed by an old man whom he vaguely recognised.

George, the groom. Was he still here?

Then an older woman appeared, and every muscle in his body tensed. He recognised her immediately, despite the greying hair. Elsa Parker—the housekeeper at Westwick the summer he'd been brought here after the accident.

He could still remember the pity shadowing her eyes that day which had made him feel so weak, so pathetic.

What the hell was she doing here? Hadn't she left years

ago? She was one of the reasons he hadn't had any intention of returning before this year. She had been kind to him that summer, but he hated that she had known him as that broken boy. And she was also the mother of the girl whose company he'd come to rely on far too much that summer.

The chasm in his stomach widened. Apparently, this damn trip was going to be even more excruciating than he had anticipated.

Tallulah stirred against him, her cornflower-blue eyes blinking open. Then she stretched and yawned. 'We're here.'

He found himself smiling despite the weight in his gut.

Dio, but even her misguided love for this miserable place enchanted him…

At least he would not have to suffer it on his own, not this time. And while Elsa Parker might remember him from that summer, she would not recognise the man he had become. He had exorcised that boy a long time ago. And he doubted she knew of his friendship with her daughter, Tali, as she had been so busy with her new responsibilities. He would have to be sure to keep the housekeeper well away from Tallulah. He didn't want his fake wife seeing that weakness or even knowing about it. The less she knew about that messed-up kid, the better.

'Come, your staff are already waiting to greet you…' he said, his voice gruff as he threaded his fingers with hers, reassured by her presence again.

How had he become so reliant on her company in such a short space of time?

She looked past him, then grinned, as the chauffeur opened the door. '*Your* staff, you mean.'

But when he climbed out of the car, and helped her out,

the strangest thing happened. Elsa Parker rushed up to Tallulah and threw her arms around her.

'Tali, you're back! How are you, love?'

Tali? The name reverberated through his consciousness. That was *her* name, the name of the child who had snuck into his room, and talked to him about everything and nothing, taking his mind off the pain, the loneliness… But who had also been there, hiding in the wardrobe, the one time his father had come to visit him. And berated him for being foolish enough to befriend a Sicilian guttersnipe—and detailed all Sante's crimes, crimes which had turned out to be lies.

He watched, in horrified slow motion, as Tallulah hugged the woman back. 'Mum, you didn't have to come and meet me. I told you I'd come to the cottage to visit this evening.'

Mum? Elsa Parker was Tallulah Whittaker's mother?

The woman he had married, the woman who had somehow broken through the barriers he had spent so long building since that summer…was also *Tali*. He remembered the girl's name. The little girl who had once seen him at his very worst, before he had been able to put those barriers in place.

The weight in his stomach plummeted, his mind reeling, the shock and anger making his heart pump so hard it felt as if it would smash through his ribs.

Suddenly, it all made a hideous kind of sense. The way he'd gravitated towards her. The way he'd come to rely on her. The way he'd trusted her so easily, *too* easily. Because it was the same thing he had done all those years ago, when he'd spent a summer in darkness and agony and had come to depend on that cheerful, cheeky child to drag him back into the light.

There had been something about her, that first day, in the library, something familiar which he had ruthlessly ignored, because it had made him feel weak. But now it was staring him in the face, impossible to ignore.

Nausea gathered in his gut, threatening to rise up his throat like bile.

He could still see her childish face, so bright, so earnest, so sweet, telling him not to be sad, that she would be his friend, while tears of humiliation stung his eyes. And the pain in his leg had been nothing compared to the agony in his heart.

Because his best friend had betrayed him and left him to die. Because his mother had been so reckless and impulsive she'd put her addictions above the needs of her own children. Because his father saw him as nothing more than a means of continuing his own sterile, pointless legacy.

They'd *all* betrayed him, but somehow, in this agonising moment, the fact Tallulah, no, *Tali*, had remained silent about who she really was, for a month, felt like the biggest betrayal of all.

She glanced over her shoulder now. But those beautiful eyes, which still had the power to destroy him, immediately saw his anguish. 'Dario, is everything okay…? I—I want to introduce you to my mum.'

He gave a stiff nod, letting his anger build to hide his panic. What a fool he'd been, to trust her. To *let* her trick him.

'We've met,' he mumbled, unable to look at the older woman.

Tallulah's eyes widened, her face flushing.

He saw the flicker of distress cross her face, but the fear was too huge, that she would see the hurt, the anguish churning in his stomach.

If only he could get back into the car, and leave, arrange to sell this place as soon as possible. He owed her nothing. She had deceived him, wormed her way into his affections, when he didn't want her there. When he'd *never* wanted *anyone* there. Ever again.

But somehow, he couldn't seem to make himself walk away. Even now, he couldn't make the clean break that would take him back to being the man he wanted to be, instead of the broken boy.

He grasped Tallulah's upper arm—acting on impulse now—and walked past her mother and the others. The varying levels of surprise and shock on their faces was nothing compared to the guilt he saw shadowing Tallulah's face…no, *Tali's* face.

'We need to talk,' he said, grinding out the words past the fury and pain as he escorted her into the house. 'About why you lied to me, *Tali*.'

'Dario, stop, you're scaring me…' Tali tried to dig her heels into the carpet as Dario marched through the house, past the salon, where the crew of decorators had already set up. Down the hallway, then up the main staircase.

She had to jog to keep up with his long strides, the limp not slowing him down much.

She hadn't expected him to even remember her mum, had convinced herself he'd forgotten them both. Because he'd never mentioned it…

But what should have pleased her, had devastation welling in her chest. Because she had seen the devastation on his face when he'd recognised her mother…and then her.

He hauled her into the library, slammed the door behind them, then grasped her other arm to force her face to his.

'You lied to me,' he said, the tone of his voice vibrating

with anger, but beneath it she could hear the panic. 'You let me marry you, let me come to rely on you, let me fuck you like my life depended on it…without ever telling me who you really were.'

She struggled out of his hold, clasping her hands over the place where his fingers had dug in, her whole body shaking with all the emotions bombarding her at once—shock, panic and anguish at his visceral reaction to discovering her identity, but topping them all was confusion.

What had she done that was so terrible? So unforgiveable?

But one thing she did know was that she hadn't lied to him.

'You never asked,' she said. 'I—I thought you'd forgotten all about me… If you must know, I was embarrassed to remind you, because it made me realise that while our friendship back then had been so important to me, it never had been to you.'

She'd loved being with him that summer. Because she'd been lonely, too. Her father had disappeared that spring, she'd had to leave all her friends behind in Dorset to live at Westwick, and every night for weeks she'd listened to her mum's wrenching sobs through the bedroom wall, not knowing what to do to make her happy again.

But then she'd discovered Dario. And every time she had made that surly boy smile, even laugh, it had felt like she had achieved a miracle. And it had helped to convince her, long after he'd gone back to boarding school, that she'd be able to fix not just her mother's sadness, but that somehow she might have fixed him, too.

He swore, in both English and Italian, then turned away from her to march to the tall, mullioned window which looked out onto the grounds.

He growled something else in Italian…the words thick with anger. But she grasped the meaning. He was accusing her of deceiving him. Of knowing who he was, of knowing all about his dysfunctional relationship with his father, because she'd witnessed it, and pretending not to know.

'What exactly was I tricking you into doing, Dario?' she asked, her voice shaking as she approached him, knowing she had to find the courage to confront him—and to stand up for herself. Because she wasn't the only one who had wanted to change the terms of their arrangement.

Perhaps she was a naïve idiot to have fallen in love with him. And yes, maybe that *was* because she had known the damaged, victimised boy, as well as the man he had made himself become. But why was he so upset that she'd been able to see past the ruthless, controlled autocrat to the caring, tender, protective, possessive man he could be…if he had ever allowed himself to need her the way she needed him.

She hadn't tricked him—not intentionally. Because *he* was the one who had always held all the power in this relationship. And *she* was the one who had fallen hopelessly in love. Yet she had *never* demanded more from him than he was willing to give her, because in some neglected part of her heart, she'd convinced herself she didn't have the right to ask.

Yes, she should have told him who she was, but the reason she hadn't was she had been scared he would look at her with the same blank expression on his face her father had given her the last time she'd seen him, before he'd walked out on her and her mother.

But whose fault was it really that she loved Dario so much now, when he had never even attempted to disguise his desire for her? Not once.

When he swung back round, his gaze was harsh, fierce, still furious.

'You tricked me into caring about you. Into needing you. More than I should. Much more than I ever wanted to.' He glanced around the library, then swore again. '*Dio*, I even considered keeping this estate that I hate, just so I could keep you...'

He spat the words at her, as if that was the greatest insult of all. And worse, as if she had been angling for that all along...as if the feelings she had tried so hard not to burden him with had been nothing more than a scheme to make him keep Westwick.

Her eyes burned with all the tears she'd never shed for that little girl, who had wanted her daddy to love her but had never understood why he couldn't. And the grown woman who had wanted to tell this man that she cared for him deeply, that she wanted more than a fake marriage but had been scared of asking too much of him, too soon.

How had she allowed herself to be so vulnerable? *Again.*

'I didn't trick you...' she said, the tears scalding her throat now as she fought like hell to hold them back. She wouldn't cry—she wouldn't *let* him make her cry. 'Do you really think I care about Westwick or my job more than I care about you? About us?'

He reared back as if she'd slapped him. The flash of panic and fear in his eyes only confirmed what he'd already told her though. He didn't *want* her to care about him. Which only made it so much harder to admit that she always had.

'I did not ask that of you. Nor do I require it.'

And there it was, the rejection she'd feared all along.

But as she tried to gather herself, to guard what was left

of her already battered heart from more pain, he added, 'This relationship can never be real.'

'Why not?' she asked, but she could see the answer she'd feared in his eyes.

'Because that is not what I want. And it never was. Not even as a boy.'

It wasn't true. She *knew* it wasn't. She had seen how lonely he had been that summer, the way he'd softened towards her over the weeks, even when he'd tried to disguise it. Even as an eight-year-old, she'd understood—he'd needed her.

But she couldn't reach this man the way she'd once been able to reach the boy.

And she would only hurt herself more now if she tried.

'You know that day your father came to visit you, I hated him so much. The awful things he said to you, the way he talked to you as if you were nothing. It was so obvious he didn't know you, that he didn't care about you…'

He stepped forward, his face rigid with rejection now. 'Don't talk about that day. I don't ever want to hear you talk about it again.'

'He hurt you, and you were already so broken…' she carried on, despite his warning tone, refusing to be silenced again. 'But you know why I recognised how broken you were?'

He didn't respond, his gaze fierce with fury.

'Because my father had already abandoned me, too.'

He flinched, and she saw a moment of regret cross his features. But that too was ruthlessly controlled. 'This has no bearing on your deception now.'

She shook her head, feeling sick inside.

'When did you become *him*, Dario?' she whispered. 'When did you close yourself off from your emotions so completely, that you believed the lies he told you about Sante? When did you convince yourself that it's better to feel nothing than to let yourself get hurt?' She gulped, because he was staring at her now as if she'd lost her mind.

She didn't care. She wasn't going to let him gaslight her and make out like she was the coward here.

'I didn't tell you I was Tali because I was convinced you didn't remember me, and you know why I was convinced about that? Because for a moment, I didn't recognise you either that day in the library.' She glanced at his scar, which flexed as he clenched his teeth. 'Oh, I knew who you were, the scars, your injured leg, but I didn't recognise the boy who could smile, who could laugh, who I'd managed to draw out of his shell… Until we were in Sicily and then Capri… But that was all just an illusion, wasn't it? You were on an endorphin high that I'd supplied.' She gulped in a painful breath, the sickness, the regret, the devastation almost more than she could bear. 'I get it now… It wasn't *me* you wanted. It was just some great recreational sex, and to get your mother's palazzo back.'

'I never promised you more…' he began, his words so terse and defensive she wanted to scream.

'No, you never did. And that's on me. But you knew every time I reached for you, every time you reached for me, that I wanted more… And on some level, you let me believe there *could* be more. You know, my dad made me think I had no value because he didn't want me. I won't let you do the same…' she declared, even though she knew in many ways she already had. Because it was going to take a very long time to repair her heart.

She threw up her hands, looking round the library she'd always loved. The place where she'd agreed to his bargain, in order to save it… The place that was tarnished now… Because it was a symbol of how stupid she'd been to think a pile of stone and mortar, however grand, however beautiful, however important to her, and the people she loved, could *ever* mean more to her than her pride and confidence and self-respect.

She'd allowed herself to fall in love with a man who'd closed off his heart a long time ago—and she'd been too starry-eyed and optimistic to truly have known she couldn't fix him too, the way she'd had the tiles on the roof repaired, or the potholes in the driveway filled.

'If you want to sell Westwick, to demolish it, I can't stop you…' she said, utterly defeated. She'd failed her colleagues, her mum, and that hurt, but she'd failed herself more. 'Because our bargain is done.'

She turned and walked away from him. He didn't say anything to stop her, the silence deafening… Somehow, she managed to keep the tears inside her, until she walked down the stairs, past the workmen, then through the hallways smelling of fresh paint. She broke into a run, though, as she passed the carriage house, where her old office was, and the flat that was no longer her home, and rounded the stables until she reached the path through the fields leading towards the woods and her mother's cottage.

She'd have to tell her mum and Ellie and George and everyone else how badly she'd fucked up, soon. But somehow losing Westwick, and everything she'd worked so hard to save by making that stupid deal with him, didn't feel as painful as losing the dreams she'd nurtured for the last few weeks—god, maybe even years—that she could be the one to scale the walls Dario Lorenti had built around his heart.

CHAPTER FIFTEEN

'I—I HAVE TO talk to everyone, tell them they're losing their j-jobs,' Tali murmured, her voice jerking through the gulping sobs she hadn't been able to contain since her mother had arrived at the cottage ten minutes ago.

'Honey, don't worry about any of that yet…' her mum said, her voice soothing, her arms tightening around her as Tali knelt by the old armchair and hugged her mum's knees, trying to gather the strength to stop crying and start planning. 'You're distraught, Tali. There's no need to…'

'There's e-every need, M-Mum.' She raised her head, forced herself to stop burying her face in her mother's lap like a child instead of a grown woman. 'Don't you see, it's all my f-fault. I've lost everyone their jobs, and you your home, because I c-couldn't get it into my stupid head that this relationship was always fake.'

Her lungs tightened with panic.

'I don't even know if he'll give them severance pay,' she said, starting to feel nauseous again. 'He was so angry with…'

'Stop!' Her mother's voice became firm, and less sympathetic. 'If it comes to that, it's out of your hands. We are all adults, and you've always taken far too much responsibility onto your shoulders for everyone here, not to mention for this estate.'

'But Mum, you'll lose this p-place and…'

'And I'll be okay. I'll find somewhere else to live, we both will,' she interrupted again. Then pressed warm hands—roughened by years of hard work—to Tali's cheeks. 'You have to stop worrying about me, sweetheart, I'm not fragile the way I was that summer. Let me look after you now, okay? Because that's *my* job, not yours.'

Tali nodded, feeling even worse. 'Okay, Mum, you're… Y-you're right. And I'm sorry.'

Why had she tried to hold everything together so tightly? Wasn't this just another example of how she had let her tendency to want to fix everyone but herself become a weakness instead of a strength?

'You have nothing to be sorry for, Tali,' her mum continued, her tone softening as she wiped away the tears still streaking down Tali's face. 'That little girl was so fierce, and so determined to make me happy again. And it worked, you know. Because I finally realised, that even though he walked away from us, he left me with you.'

Tali bowed her head, blindsided by her overwrought emotions again.

'But you know, Tali, I'm not sure all this guilt over Westwick is even warranted anyway.'

'How so?' Tali asked.

'From the look on Mr Lorenti's face before he realised who you were, I don't think it was fake for him either…'

'Please don't, Mum.' Tali stood up to get away from her mum's misguided attempts to make her feel better.

She swiped the last of the tears off her raw cheeks as she walked to the window that looked out on the woods. The thunderous rainstorm, which had begun not long after she'd got to the cottage two hours ago, was somehow a perfect refection of her misery. Her ribs started to ache, alongside her heart, because that blasted bubble of hope hadn't entirely died and she needed it to now. Whatever her mum had thought she'd seen in Dario's expression, she'd been wrong. Just like Tali had.

God, what was it about them both that they still had the ability to romanticise a man's reaction after they'd both been so comprehensively slam-dunked by love?

'I expect he's halfway back to London by now,' she said, trying not to imagine him in the limo alone, with that blank look on his face—which had been worse than his fury. 'Busy ordering his real estate division to find a buyer…' she added. *Or figuring out if he can have Westwick demolished*, she thought miserably, the sickening feeling—of how badly she'd messed things up by falling in love with her fake husband—working its way up her chest again to strangle her. She didn't try to swallow it down this time, though, because she needed to feel the pain if she was ever going to get over him.

'He didn't leave, you know. He was still in the library looking morose. I found him there twenty minutes ago after searching the place for you both.'

Tali swung around, shocked at the news. It had been nearly two hours since she'd left the Hall… And she knew he hated to spend any time here—it had been obvious as soon as he'd agreed to accompany her here that he hadn't wanted to come back. Just another reason why she'd started to convince herself he might actually care for her…

But then she forced herself to breathe through her latest delusion.

It was pissing down outside. He had probably just decided to stay put until the weather cleared. Knowing he was still so close, though, was a whole new form of torture.

She was about to say as much to her mother when a loud rap on the front door made them both jump.

'Who could that be in this weather?' her mother asked, heading past her to the front door.

But when she flung it open, and Tali saw Dario standing on the doorstep, his designer suit soaked through, his eyes as dark as the storm clouds outside, her heart went into free fall… As it plunged to earth, about to crash and burn all over again, he stepped over the threshold, dripping onto the doormat and asked her mother, in a low voice, 'Signora Parker, please may I speak with your daughter alone?'

Before Tali could detach her gaze long enough to tell her mum she couldn't speak to Dario, not again, because she wasn't sure she could keep hold of the few morsels of pride she had left and not throw herself at him this time—when he looked so sad, so tortured, so alone—her mum closed the door behind him and said, 'I'll go and fold the laundry upstairs and leave you two, but you need to understand one thing, Mr Lorenti.'

He blinked as if he were trying to wake himself from a coma, his gaze raking over Tali with an intensity that was making her skin heat despite the pain.

But then he turned, to address her mother. '*Sì*, Signora Parker.'

'If you hurt her again, I'll have to murder you, even if it means Westwick is lost forever.'

He nodded, slowly. 'Understood.'

And then her mother was gone. Tali's heart was in pieces, but she wasn't sure anymore whether it was still broken or about to mend. Because Dario didn't look furious with her anymore, and he didn't look indifferent either… He looked shattered, too.

Was it possible that by finally standing her ground, finally telling him what she needed, he'd realised that he needed it, too?

Dario limped across the small room, his head nearly butting the exposed beams, towards Tallulah. His leg was killing him, the vicious spring storm and the trudge through the muddy fields as he'd searched for the cottage having cramped the ruined muscles—but something about the pain and the grim weather suited his mood perfectly.

He deserved to be in agony. He deserved to be punished. After the things he'd said, the things he'd threatened to do. All simply to protect himself, from this woman who… as soon as she had stood up to him and called him out on all his bullshit, he had finally understood he couldn't live without.

How had he managed to lie to himself for weeks?

She stepped away from him as he got closer, tearing his heart right out of his chest.

He had done this. He had hurt her so badly she did not love him anymore. But maybe he could still salvage this situation. Maybe he could still keep her, make her love him again…if he begged. Funny to think that begging someone to care for him—letting them see all his weaknesses and vulnerabilities—had always been the thing he had been most terrified of, but it wasn't anymore… Because not doing so would mean losing Tallulah.

'Dario, why are you here?' she finally whispered, her face a picture of…*what*? Was that panic, disgust, shock? Why could he not read her expression anymore?

She stared at him, those luminous blue eyes making

the regret and guilt slice through him like a knife, because he could see no hate in her eyes when there should have been—only compassion. Was this good? Or was she just too kind a person to hate anyone—even him?

He clung to the thought, though, desperate to believe he hadn't destroyed his chance completely.

'I came to say I'm sorry,' he said, his voice breaking on the inadequate word. 'I want another chance.'

'A ch-chance for what?' she said, but then her eyes grew round, and the hurt shadowing them had the knife twisting in his gut. 'If you need this marriage to get ownership of your palazzo, y-you don't have to divorce me yet, but I can't be with you, not anymore, you must understand that… It's too painful for me.'

Hope swelled against his ribs, hope he didn't deserve but would grab with both hands.

He brushed his thumb over the reddened skin of her cheek, disgusted with himself when she flinched.

'I already own the palazzo,' he said. 'The legal transfer of ownership was completed yesterday.'

'You…wh-what?' she asked, the transparent expression—confusion and concern—almost as beautiful as she was to him.

'I didn't tell you because I did not want you to leave me.'

'But…'

He cupped her cheeks in his palms, grateful that she did not flinch again. Pressing his fingers into her silky curls, he drew her into his body. He held her, stroking the soft skin, needing to breath in her ragged breaths, needing to share this connection, which had always felt so visceral, so right, so perfect, even though he had tried so hard never to acknowledge how much it meant to him.

He must confess everything now and place himself at her mercy.

'I see now, what I should have realised the first time we made love…' He swore softly when she shuddered. He was doing this wrong. 'No, the first time I kissed you.' He lifted his forehead from hers, stared into those bright, luminous, honest eyes and forced himself to be honest, too. 'No, the first time I touched you… That I wanted more from you, too.'

Her brow furrowed, but her hands flattened against his waist, her fingers curling into his wet shirt. 'Do you really mean that, Dario? Please don't lie to me again.'

'I have been so lonely, for so long. I thought…' He swallowed, controlling the familiar panic, forcing himself to tell her the truth. 'I thought if I owned the palazzo, it would be enough. But I don't want to be there without you,' he replied, without hesitation this time, without anger, without cowardice. 'I know now, it was never my safe place, that was always you. Even when you were Tali, and not Tallulah, you were the only person who ever made me feel unbroken. I'm sorry it took me so long to admit the truth to myself as well as you.'

'Dario…' she whispered, but the sadness remained in her eyes when she pressed a trembling palm to his scarred cheek. 'I want to believe that so much. But I'm scared… You shut me out. And that hurt. I want to be with you too, to see if we can make this a real relationship but I can't…'

'Shhh…' He held her face up to his. Pressed his lips to hers. 'It is already real, Tallulah.' Taking her palm from his cheek, he pressed it against his wet shirt. 'Do you feel how hard my heart is beating?'

She nodded, her eyes widening, the love in them so transparent he felt humbled.

'That is because I am scared, too,' he said, finally forced to admit his greatest fear. 'In fact, I am terrified, that I have messed this up so badly—by not trusting you, by accusing you of things you did not do to protect myself—you will decide you do not love me after all.'

'Don't be scared, because I do,' she said with such courage it humbled him even more.

How could it be so easy? he thought. All he had had to do was trust his feelings, to trust her love, and she'd let him back in.

The pain in his heart lifted as he clasped her head and covered her mouth with his, devouring her sweet lips, feeding the surge of desire and letting himself be swept away on the wave of love.

When they were finally forced to break apart, to breathe, she whispered, 'Does this mean we're really married?'

'*Absolutamente*,' he said, and then sealed their deal with another kiss.

EPILOGUE

Two years later

'BRACE YOURSELF, here comes chaos,' Dario murmured in Tali's ear, his arm tightening around her shoulders as she waved enthusiastically while they watched Sante and Mia's large black SUV drive into the palazzo's forecourt—three hours late.

She laughed, delighted by his stern expression and the heat in his eyes. 'Oh, shut up, and stop pretending you don't enjoy the chaos when they're here,' she whispered out of the corner of her mouth.

'And yet, I am also equally delighted when they are gone again!' he said, but she could hear the amusement in his voice.

Mia popped out of the passenger seat, followed by two dogs who bounded up to them in a melee of delighted yips and barks and wagging tales. Mia's round belly made the fierce hugs she gave them both—amid a tumble of profuse apologies for the delay—almost as chaotic as the dogs' excited welcome.

Sante meanwhile jumped out from the driver's side, to lift his baby daughter, Ariana, out of her car seat in the back and carry her over to join the welcoming party—

the baby apparently totally unflustered by all the noise and activity.

'Oh wow, she's grown so much!' Tali remarked, reaching out to take the blinking toddler into her arms. 'How old is she now?' she asked, even though she already knew the answer.

Sante's chest puffed up with pride as he stroked his daughter's fluffball of hair. 'Thirteen months and *finally* sleeping through the night!' he said with mock exasperation. 'Mostly.'

'Just in time for this one to arrive in two months' time and keep us up all night instead,' announced Mia as she stroked her stomach.

'And whose fault is that?' demanded Dario, going into big-brother mode. 'What were you two thinking getting pregnant again so soon after Ariana was born?'

Mia sent him a cheeky grin. 'It wasn't exactly planned, Dario,' she said, at the same time as her husband murmured, 'It is certainly not my fault your sister is irresistible, Dario.'

'*Dio*, Sante!' Dario said, covering his ears, while the dogs continued to prance around them and Ariana started to cry. 'Do not talk to me about my sister like that…'

'Hey, you're the one that started it,' Sante replied, the smile on his face one that made Tali smile, too.

She jostled Ariana on her hip until the baby stopped crying, while the staff arrived to transport the insane amount of luggage from the car to the apartment Tali and Dario had had decorated over a year ago, so Mia and her family could visit the palazzo whenever they wished.

The two men continued to talk on the patio, while she and Mia headed into the house.

It was so good to hear them joking with each other.

After a shaky start, Dario and Sante had become good friends again. Buddies even. And she loved to see it. For Dario most of all… After having no one close in his life, he now had three people—four if you counted the niece she knew he adored—who would always be there for him.

'Here, let me take her, she's tired, I should put her down for a nap,' Mia suggested, because Ariana was still niggling.

'It's okay, I've got her,' Tali said, loving the warm weight of the little girl in her arms, and the smell of baby shampoo that clung to her. The pang of longing in her chest was hard to deny. 'Let's take her to her room,' she said.

It didn't take the two of them long to get Ariana ready for her nap. Tali changed her and gave her a bottle while her mother directed the staff where to put all the luggage.

After burping her, Tali placed her into the crib and watched with tears stinging her eyes as the baby rolled over and dropped into sleep almost instantly.

'She's so gorgeous,' she murmured, the wave of raw emotion making her lungs hurt.

She blinked furiously, to stop the ridiculous tears from falling. She thought she'd got away with it, but as soon as they had tiptoed out of the room and Mia had closed the door softly, her sister-in-law's eyes narrowed.

'Okay, spill it, what's going on? You look exhausted, Tali. And as adorable as I find my daughter, she doesn't usually make people look as if they're about to burst into tears.'

Tali choked out a laugh. She couldn't help it, even as she felt the twinge of panic.

She should have spoken to Dario about this a week ago. She'd bought the pregnancy test five days ago now, and hadn't had the guts to use it, convinced her period was bound to happen any moment. She'd had her coil removed, a month ago, and the doctor had mentioned they should wait seven days or use other forms of contraceptive after she'd starting using a contraceptive patch, just to be on the safe side. But they hadn't…*quite*…and now she was more than a week late. And she still didn't know how to bring up the conversation.

They'd talked about having children—of course they had. But only in a vague, we're-both-on-board-with-the-concept-eventually kind of way. While she knew Dario had been joking with Mia and Sante when they arrived, she also knew he was a man who liked to plan things out. So did she, really.

But they'd been so busy over the last few days, finishing up their work commitments to make time for this two-week visit… And this morning, when she'd planned to tell him she was a bit late, and probably should take a test, before she could mention it, he'd started kissing her and well…they'd got sidetracked, completely.

Seriously, who am I kidding?

The truth was she was a total coward. She didn't want to tell Dario, in case he wasn't as overjoyed about the prospect of a pregnancy as she was.

'I think I might be pregnant…' she blurted, as the words she should have said to Dario first popped out without warning.

Mia's eyebrows shot up her forehead, but then a smile beamed across her face. 'Oh. My. God. This is wonderful. Why didn't you two tell us when…'

'Because Dario doesn't know, yet,' Tali interrupted Mia's excited response. 'And neither do I, really,' she added, the guilt starting to cripple her now. 'I haven't taken the test yet. It's still in my bedside drawer. In fact,

I haven't even got up the guts to tell him I'm a week late. I feel like such a…'

'Whoa, whoa, whoa…' Mia grasped her hands, then slung an arm around her shoulders to pull her into a tight hug. 'Breathe, Tali. It's okay.'

She drew in a careful breath and let Mia hold her, the hug comforting, and somehow reassuring.

'I don't know what's wrong with me. I'm probably not even pregnant,' she started to babble. 'It's just…as soon as I realised I *might* be pregnant, I wanted to be, *so much*. But what if Dario doesn't feel the same way? What if he's not ready yet…'

'Shush, it's okay…' Mia placed warm palms on Tali's cheeks and smiled at her, managing to calm her rampaging heartbeat, at least a little. 'Really, Tali, the only way to find that out is to ask him.'

'I know it's silly, but…'

'And honestly, I think he'll be overjoyed at the prospect.'

'You do?' Tali said, still unsure, still not wanting to hope too much.

The last two years had been like a dream—a dream she never wanted to wake up from. Of course, they'd had their disagreements. Dario was bossy and demanding, and he liked to have things all his own way. So, she'd had to discover her kickass side, and fast—particularly when he'd suggested she give up her job and move full-time to Italy. It hadn't always been easy to make their marriage work, but after some heated arguments, and lots of debate—and no small amount of make-up sex—they'd found a compromise. They divided their time now between Wiltshire and Milan and Capri, both of them working remotely when required. And she loved their life. She wasn't sure how a baby was going to fit into that, if there was one. The only thing she was absolutely sure of was that her mum would be overjoyed to be a granny. But she wanted to face the challenge of starting a family with Dario. She knew he would be a wonderful dad—just watching him with Ariana had proved that. But what if he wasn't as sure?

He'd let his guard down with her. And she knew he trusted her. But she also knew he still found it hard sometimes to be open about his feelings, to share and discuss—after a lifetime of being scared to show a weakness. And she was even more scared that if he didn't want this 'possible' baby, he wouldn't want to tell her how he really felt, for fear of losing her. Even though she'd told him so many times that would never happen.

'Yes, I do,' Mia said, with a confidence Tali wanted to feel, too. 'He adores you, Tali. And he'd make a great dad… Probably way too overprotective of course, but I'm afraid you'll have to deal with that. Then again, I've managed to stop Sante from freaking out over every minor hiccup, usually on very little sleep, so I'm sure you can do the same for my big brother.'

Tali laughed, the first genuine laugh she'd managed in over a week.

Mia was right. Of course she was. She was working herself into a tizzy for no reason.

'Listen,' Mia murmured, rubbing Tali's arms. 'Why don't I go downstairs and send him up so you can take that test together? Sante and I have to get unpacked anyway, and settle Romulus and Remus, before Dario has them both evicted,' she added, rolling her eyes comically because they could still hear the dogs barking intermittently downstairs.

'Okay,' Tali managed, but she could still feel her stomach going into free fall as Mia headed off with an encouraging smile on her face.

'Mia said you needed to talk to me in private.' Dario walked into the bedroom suite, his stomach flipping over and his heart hammering his chest wall.

Something was wrong. He'd known it for days. And when Mia had arrived on the terrazzo and told him—with no small amount of drama—his wife needed to speak to him, it had started to scare him.

Why the hell hadn't he said something sooner? Discovered what the problem was? He'd noticed her silences, those far-off looks, the strange expression he had been unable to decipher because he hadn't seen it before. Not exactly panic, but not the sweet, uncomplicated happiness he was used to seeing. And she'd been so tired in the past few days. Most mornings she rose before he did—but not in the past week. And while he'd enjoyed the extra time to snuggle with her, now he was questioning that, too.

He had no idea what this something was. But when she turned towards him, her hands clasped so tightly the knuckles had whitened, it didn't just scare him anymore—it terrified him.

He crossed the room in a few strides, gripped her hands until they stopped shaking, then laid his palm on her cheek.

'What is it, Tallulah? Whatever it is, we can fix it,' he said, the panic starting to consume him, because he could see the sheen of tears in her eyes now, too.

He watched her throat contract as she swallowed, bracing for the worst, when she whispered, 'I need to take a pregnancy test.'

He stilled—the sudden rush of joy so strong, it was almost impossible to contain.

He had wanted to speak of babies for months now. Especially when she had had the coil removed. The suggestion that she not get the contraceptive patch had been on the tip of his tongue. He wanted to see her round with his child, to see her become a mother, to see her blossom and shine, to see her nurture his baby at her breast. God, he wanted all of it. He'd even been jealous of Sante, for having a beautiful daughter and another baby on the way…

But he knew his wife loved her job—in fact, they'd had more than a few arguments about her keeping the position at Westwick in the early days of their real marriage. Once he'd realised how important it was to her, though, he knew he couldn't pressure her into starting a family too soon.

So, he forced his features to remain impassive now. It was harder than he thought, even though he had had a lifetime of practice at keeping his emotions on lockdown, until he had met Tallulah.

'Okay?' he said. 'Do you want me to get Angelo to acquire one from *la farmacia*?'

'I already have one, I've had it for a week. Because I'm a week late.'

He nodded, not sure what that meant. But then she blinked, and a tear rolled down her cheek—which felt like a knife to his gut.

'You are not happy to have my baby?' he asked, his usually fluent English deserting him.

She shook her head. But then a watery smile spread across her lips. 'You—you're not unhappy at the prospect of us having an unplanned pregnancy?'

He placed his hand on her flat stomach. '*Dio*, no,' he said, the joy rushing through him as the smile in her eyes made the tears sparkle and glow. 'There's nothing I want more in this world than to see you have my child.'

She laughed, the sound echoing joyously in his heart, as she threw herself into his arms and he caught her. Then she whispered against his neck. 'Ditto.'

Ten minutes later, when the extra line appeared on the test stick, he swung her around, then kissed her senseless.

It was a long while later before they managed to make it downstairs to tell Mia and Sante the good news—and ring Tallulah's mother in Wiltshire. Dario was so overjoyed at the prospect of becoming a father, he didn't even mind that Sante spent the rest of the evening mocking him for failing to properly plan his *own* family.

'Sometimes, brother, planning is overrated,' Dario declared, slapping his old friend on the shoulder. 'And now, I can't wait for the chaos to begin!'

* * * * *

If you just couldn't get enough of
Boss's Bride Price,
then be sure to check out the
previous instalment in the Enemy Tycoons duet,
Enemies Until After Hours
by Natalie Anderson!

And why not explore these other stories
by Heidi Rice?

Queen's Winter Wedding Charade
Princess for the Headlines
Billionaire's Wedlocked Wife
The Heir Affair
Greek's Kidnapped Princess

Available now!